Wildfire in the Desert

Wildfire in the Desert

by

Bruno Jambor

www.penmorepress.com

Wildfire in The Desert by Bruno Jambor
Copyright © 2015 Bruno Jambor

ISBN: 978-1-942756-06-4   Paperback
ISBN: 978-1-942756-07-1   Ebook

BISAC Subject Headings:
FIC002000 FICTION / Action & Adventure
FIC022080FICTION / Mystery & Detective /
FIC050000FICTION / Crime

Address all correspondence to:
M James
920 N Javelina Pl.
Tucson, AZ 85748
Or visit our website at:
www.PenmorePress.com

Dedication

To my wife, Pat, who loves the stars, the desert, and history as much as I do.

When the past no longer illuminates the future,
the spirit walks in darkness.
— Alexis de Tocqueville

Chapter 1

It was an answer to his deepest yearning, a real celestial favor. Nothing could be better than being alone in the desert, high on the slope of Baboquivari Mountain. Manuel lifted his glass to the heavens in thanksgiving and savored the mescal slowly, the way he liked it, pure, nothing but fermented juice of burnt agave.

As he put down his glass, he caught sight of a pickup truck hell bent on destroying its suspension on the steep, rough road that dead ended at his house. He recognized his nephew, Rodrigo. It had to be important. Unless absolutely driven by necessity, his nephew avoided him.

Stopping in a squeal of brakes, the driver jumped out, tried to slam the door behind him, missed the door handle, and ran toward his uncle with a scowling face.

"You have a mountain lion chasing you?" started Manuel.

"Tio, do me a favor."

"You need money?"

"I'm in trouble. I'll leave something here with you. The police got tipped off and are waiting for me at my house. I got a call from somebody I work with. He said to get rid of the merchandise immediately. If they catch me I'm in for ten years, at least! Help me! I've got to leave the stuff here. Nobody'll suspect it's here. They respect you too much."

"Whoa! Stop yakking like a cactus wren! Can't make sense of it! What merchandise? What are you hauling in your truck?"

"It's... well, it's... you know, that's how I make money to survive."

"What?"

"Come on, don't be stupid, Tio. It's... Oh hell! Do I have to tell you? OK, it's pot. The police are after me. I have to stash it here for a few days... just until things go quiet. They mustn't find it or I'm done for."

Manuel looked at the young man—blue jeans, jean vest, boots, big leather belt with a phone and a small knife in a leather pouch hanging from it. He could see perspiration above the lip that was adorned with a thin, well groomed mustache. How old was he, exactly? Close to twenty-five now? He was short of breath.

"Peace! Rodrigo, pipe down. Who else knows you're here?"

"Nobody! I told my informer I was turning back south and would hide it near San Miguel. I have to hide it pronto. Every minute counts. As I told you, police are looking for me at my house. If I'm too late, they'll figure out that I'm on to them and come looking for me. I've got to get home fast and clean. You're right here where I can dump it, and adios, I'm gone. Please, Tio, help me. You've got to do me this favor."

So much for celestial favors. This was more like a nightmare. A trap waited for him in this proposal. "Maybe the pen would do you good! You need to get your head straight. And you told this informer you'll hide the merchandise?"

"Tio, don't play stupid games. I need you. If you love me, Tio, you won't let me down."

Something in the tone of his nephew's voice struck a chord in Manuel's heart. "If you love me..." He had been a very distant uncle. Gone for years, he never wrote, never called. When he'd come back and settled in his people's land, on the side of Baboquivari Mountain, he'd learned that his sister had died and the boy's father had gone to Phoenix more than a decade ago, and there he had dropped off from everybody's radar screen. Manuel tried to help the boy, who lived with his paternal grandmother, herself in her late eighties at the time. Rodrigo did not want any help. Manuel tried to make peace with him by occasionally offering him small sums of money that the boy took without any gratitude. That was his easy way of showing he cared for his nephew—convenient, distant, and occasional. Manuel had kept up this mercantile relationship over the years. Now he was called to show love for this nephew and risk going to the pen with him for drug trafficking.

Manuel hesitated. This love the boy so casually requested was risky, compromising, implicating him for a lifetime. He should grab the boy, turn him around and kick his butt with a sharp-toed cowboy boot. Instead, he grabbed Rodrigo and hugged him, not knowing exactly what to do next. This was not the favor he had asked heaven for. He realized how tall the boy had grown, now just a few inches shorter than himself. Rodrigo was shaking in his arms.

"What else can I do in this lousy place? No other jobs around here. Doing this, I make money. Help me get out of this mess just once, Tio!"

Manuel made a quick decision. He was going to help temporarily until he could figure out what was best for all sides. This was the first time Rodrigo had ever asked him for help. He had to act fast.

He told the boy to unload his cargo outside the house, on the ground. He was appalled at the quantity. "How much of this damned stuff you got here?"

"Two hundred kilos.

"Two hundred!"

"What are you going to do with it?"

"You don't ask questions. You get going."

The pickup sped away and disappeared in the valley of the saguaro forest below.

Manuel wasted no time. He turned his own truck around and loaded it with the merchandise. Rodrigo's consignment goods weighed down the vehicle. He shifted into four wheel drive, lowest gear, and drove no more than five hundred yards straight up the mountain side, negotiating some very tight passages between enormous boulders. Reaching a little ledge, he set the parking brake, got out and wedged a rock behind each rear tire to hold the truck on the steep incline. He reached for a Navy duffle bag on the passenger seat and loaded it with about twenty-five kilos. Lugging the load, he disappeared behind a big rock. He reappeared ten minutes later and repeated the process until the truck bed was empty. He threw his bag back on the passenger seat and with his right hand massaged his lower back. "Damn that sobrino of mine! I must be getting old.... Two hundred kilos! I can't believe this."

He backed and turned his truck carefully around. He looked at the valley below. The desert appeared uninhabited. The sun was getting lower in the sky. His eyes followed the road far away, toward Sells, where a few houses could be seen amongst the saguaros.

Was this the end of his peaceful life? A gesture of compassion toward his nephew dispelled his dream of withdrawing from the mad world below, plunging them both into a cat and mouse game with drug cartels and police.

Back at the house, he walked around a bit to kick away the truck's tracks in the dust, then sat down under the ramada to think things over.

Suddenly a dust tail plumed above the road his nephew had

taken. As the vehicle came around the first switchback, he could make out the markings of the Tohono O'odham Police on its side. He had expected the visit. It had not taken very long. Two men were in the patrol car. His pulse quickened perceptibly.

Better them than La Migra. He knew all the men in the police force. He went in and returned with two bottles of beer from the cooler. Thus armed, he waited for them and addressed them as they approached. "Well! If it isn't Cesar and Paulo! Welcome, my friends. I saw you coming with your tongues hanging out and prepared drinks for you." He extended the bottles toward the visitors.

"You know that we never drink while on the job, Manuel," said Cesar, as he took one. Paulo was already downing the cold beer to clear his throat of the choking dust.

"So what brings you all the way up here? You want to watch the sunset with me?" asked Manuel.

"Well, yes, of course, but we also want to pay you a visit, amigo, and have a little talk," said Paulo, wiping his lips on his forearm. "You don't have many visitors up here, do you, compadre?"

"More than you think, muchacho. Just a while ago my sobrino, Rodrigo, came to say hello to me. You see, I'm not lonely."

"What did he want?" probed Cesar with subtlety.

"Why do you ask?"

"Oh, let's say we want to know if he left you a gift after he left."

"How could he leave me a gift after he left?"

"OK, smart burro, did he give you something when he was here?"

"You look like you're hunting for something. What is it?" asked Manuel.

"Maybe coyotes," started Paulo. "You know the traffic of emigrantes through here, and how many of them carry drugs to pay the coyotes. Well, basta! We suspect Rodrigo's involved with drugs."

"So why talk to me, amigo? I'm involved in it too?"

"Don't take it like that, hermano! We're just doing an investigation. We saw Rodrigo at his house. He didn't have what we were looking for. Can we take a look in your casita?"

"What are you looking for?"

"Two hundred kilos of drugs. We have reason to believe your sobrino had that much in his possession. He must have stashed it somewhere. We would like to search your house. Can we do it friendly-like, without all the damn paper work?"

Manuel exclaimed in feigned amazement, "Madre mia! Two hundred kilos! Be my guests. I cannot refuse you anything, you know it."

"Gracias, amigo!"

Cesar and Paulo disappeared inside.

Perched high above the valley, the house rested on a small, flat area that could barely accommodate the house, the ramada, and a driveway big enough to park two or three cars. A steep slope started right behind it with a long dangerous climb toward the Baboquivari Peak. Huge boulders perched a few hundred yards above the house, ready to roll down and obliterate it in a few seconds at the least earth tremor. From there the view to the south was clear all the way to the Mexican border beyond San Miguel. The Baboquivari wash tumbled dizzyingly down westward to join the Vamori wash. Between the house and the slope, a tiny shed shaded his motorcycle. Perched on top of the shed, a satellite dish connected the hermitage to the outside world.

The first room was the kitchen and dining room. It had a

large window with a view to the ramada outside and the Baboquivari valley underneath. The room had a small table and two chairs, a sink, a refrigerator, a gas stove, and some cooking and eating utensils on two shelves fixed onto the wall. In the back were a bedroom and a library. The bed was made of aspen logs and weighed a ton. "Where did you find aspen logs around here?" asked Paulo. He looked underneath and saw only old shoes at first. Then he saw a large object in a bag. He grabbed it. It was light and emitted a hollow sound.

"Watch out for my guitar, you two!" yelled Manuel, who heard the sound from outside. Paulo pushed the guitar back under the bed, disappointed. The library consisted of three large book shelves made of ancient mesquite wood, with books stacked apparently at random. How can he read so much? Paulo wondered. Next to the shelves on a table were a laptop with two speakers and a small box full of CDs. Paulo looked at some of the titles—classical music. Manuel must be a strange cat, maybe a bit loco.

Cesar had finished the inspection of the kitchen, having managed to drop only two frying pans in the process. The house was small and it took only ten minutes to go through it thoroughly. Both men emerged together, smiling to cover a bit of disappointment and at the same time relieved to have exonerated their compadre. They walked through the shed together and came back.

The first lights blinked in the distance toward Sells, signaling the coming night. They decided to shorten their visit. "So where's the stash of drugs, hermano?" joked Paulo.

"I smoked it all before you two got here."

"Remember to invite us next time," suggested Cesar, laughing.

Cesar sat behind the wheel and started the car. Manuel held the door for Paulo while he got in and looked in the back seat where a rack held a shining sniper rifle. Manuel whistled admiringly, "You go hunting for jackrabbits with this little popgun you have in the back?"

"It's meant for two-legged coyotes. Actually it's not even an equalizer if we come across drug traffickers. Their arsenal puts us to shame. But this baby is definitely going to help us some day, if we get in trouble with them."

"Who's the marksman? Is it you, Paulito?"

"Sure is!" cut in Cesar. "Your little Paulito here can hit a rattler's tail from two hundred yards. Don't ever get between him and a target."

After a few minutes of small talk they departed, pulling their dust tail behind them.

Manuel did not sleep peacefully that night. His lower back complained as he tossed around, vainly seeking the magic position that would open the door to deep sleep.

He walked out into the freshness of the starry night.

The Sonoran desert was calm this early morning in November. High in the western sky, Orion dazzled the eyes with its brilliance. Manuel walked slowly, avoiding the branches of cholla cacti invading both sides of the starlit trail. A distant yap signaled the presence of coyotes on the prowl. He reached the edge of the gully where he could survey the desert far to the west and south, and sat down on a rock near a saguaro. A mass of air, dislodged from the top of the mountain, slid along the slope and shook ever so gently the two extended branches that resembled human arms raised toward the stars. The saguaro sighed at this breath of cool air descending the bajada, and caressed it with its needles.

A lifetime of preserving his separateness from the crowds was now damaged by the foolish weakness of an instant. His goal of independence barely attained, he had taken on a role of mediator in a game that was not his own. What a costly choice the challenge to love had been, overpowering his comfort and enjoyment. Their common good demanded the surrender of his own. Yet with sacrificing his independence came a mysterious promise of freedom, a widening of his own narrow plans.

In the darkness of the gully, two saguaro trunks, washed down by summer rains, lay one atop the other like two bodies cut down by a hail of bullets. He would have to maneuver carefully to avoid a similar fate for the two of them.

He glanced at the starry sky. Orion, dagger hanging from his belt, illuminated the darkness. Like a diamond brooch in a jewel box, the Pleiades wheeled closer to the distant Mesquite Mountains at the western edge of the Tohono O'odham lands, with the Ajo range beyond. Does Orion know where he is going? he wondered. Does he walk with confidence, or is he worried like me, carrying in my gut the frustration of the man lost in the desert, turning in circles before falling down to the ground a last time, the dust of his bones to be turned into desert pavement?

Inevitably, his thoughts returned to his rash action. Why risk his accomplishment for a nephew who didn't seem to care a whit for him?

Born on the Tohono O'odham reservation, he had returned to his roots after a long absence and planted himself on the side of the Baboquivari Mountain, the legendary resting place of I'itoi, father and benefactor of the Tohono O'odham. He had lovingly built his little adobe house with mud and straw bricks individually made by hand. As member of the board of the Tohono O'odham Electric Utility Authority, he dealt with the supply of power to Kitt Peak National Astronomical Observatory, a few miles north of Baboquivari. He had few needs. The most pressing one was his need for solitude. His life long experience had taught him that peace comes with separation from others.

While in the Navy, in San Diego, he had fought to gain recognition and rise in the ranks. Each step was won at the price of having to defeat stiff competition and sometimes fierce opposition. He had to eliminate obstacles by any means. Success required the surrender of his conscience, disregarding the choices made, often at the expense of others. He had to win. It was a war, not peace.

Then, in his fiftieth year, a revulsion seized him. He quit his job, sold his house, cashed his savings, signed up for retirement benefits, and bought the motorcycle of his dreams. Up and down the west coast he rode, all the way to Vancouver and back. After the coast, he traversed the desert. He visited all the places, from Boron and Barstow to El Centro and Blythe, that had hot Mexican food and cold beer. One day in Yuma, Arizona, the urge to put an end to the emptiness of his life seized him. He felt a tingling in his spine, like that of a ten year old boy waiting for Christmas gifts to be distributed. He filled the tank with gas, opened the throttle wide, and roared into Tucson. From there, he went fifty miles southwest, home to his birthplace in the Tohono O'odham nation's land. The prodigal son had come home and he never left again.

Orion the warrior had moved. His dog Sirius at his heel, he was now high above the Ajo Mountains hunting for prey.

Manuel, the warrior in the desert, had learned peace in isolation. Now it was war again. He had, over the years spent in solitude, felt a peace given to him as a "celestial favor", as his childhood hero, Eusebio Francisco Kino, the legendary founder of the Mission San Xavier Del Bac, the White Dove of the Desert, used to say. The Jesuit's fame as a man of both science and faith—astronomer, cartographer, and explorer as well as a priest—inspired him to study at the mission school and to do better than his peers in mathematics and geography. He read all the books about his hero's life, especially one he remembered as being rather large and detailed whose title he now forgot. He obtained it on special loan from a high school in Tucson. He stayed up late many nights, reading until he could hear the first birds stirring before dawn.

He could still remember the saga of epic rides on the Camino Del Diablo, the excitement of Kino viewing the Sea of Cortez through a spyglass, his discovery that California was not an island, as it was thought to be until that time. He thrilled as Kino and his Spanish companions celebrated the victory of Pima Chief Coro over the Apaches, victory that secured the frontier between the San Pedro River and the Huachuca Mountains. He had in his veins the blood of those men who had welcomed Kino, built missions under his direction, farmed with seeds and animals brought from Spain. There was a real success story. Yet even the missions were now forgotten. Even the White Dove of the Desert was more of a museum than a force that could move people.

What was best now? Orion the hero, remote, inaccessible in the sky? Or Kino, surrounded by his converts and risking his life to protect them? A dueling contest of musical themes glowed in him. They played alternately inside his breast. He loved both but he would have to choose one—the one that would help him to solve his conundrum. On one side, the sounds of Mahler's Fifth Symphony's adagietto movement, slow, with its soaring, searing strings offered his soul self-soothing themes by sealing it from the surrounding world. For a long time this had been his favorite piece of music. It reassured him that his choice of solitude and self-determination was the right one. With a throbbing full orchestra, it was Orion's voice, that of the hero.

On the other side, a quiet, confident chant in Latin, the

"Resurrexi" of the Paschal Introit, with its successive waves inciting the hearer to open one's soul to celestial favors tailored as answers to specific events. Since his childhood he had not been attracted to liturgies. But recently he'd heard this chant and could not put it out of his mind. He bought the recording and played it often. Once discovered, it kept calling him back. It was so different. The chant asked for a sort of abandon to the rhythm even though he could not easily follow the words. The melody was able to suggest the meaning without the words. It infused a peace that brought him back to his youth and to Kino. Lately he could not decide which was better—his own hard won peace in isolation, or the serenity he experienced by simply listening to the chant. More and more, he attributed his well-being to the celestial favors so dear to his childhood hero. A music without measure, submerging uncertainty under an unknown power. That was Kino's voice.

Survival would depend on the correct choice, the appropriate attitude of the soul with its own music. A flight to heroic heights of solitude, or a journeying with others, forming a choir singing in unison, directed by a gentle hand motion. His inclination was toward the heights of isolation. But there was no room there for Rodrigo, and he would have to abandon him. After his decisive intervention, he felt he owed him more than that. On the other hand, he might need a few more voices to create a choir for the chant. Kino's voice had been still for a few centuries, yet he was the one who knew about celestial favors, who could really teach him. And wasn't there danger in sharing his secret with others? Could he even share it with Rodrigo? The secret of chanting was in the unifying motion of the musical rhythm, joined to the words pronounced by the singers. Could he pronounce the words that would reveal where he hid Rodrigo's merchandise? Throbbing staccato, or gently flowing rhythm? How to choose?

A high pitched voice in the distance yanked him out of his quandary. Other voices joined in. The coyote choir tried to unite their voices but ended with a series of yaps.

Manuel slowly retraced his steps to his house. Orion was setting. Dawn was near.

He would have to revisit Kino's words and learn again from him how to unite with the choir, how to read the ebb and flow of celestial favors.

Chapter 2

Eusebio Francisco Kino extended his hand to touch the painting he had brought with him, rolled in a leather tube leaning against the wall of the little hut that was going to be his temporary headquarters. A beautiful work of art, given to him by a friend in Mexico City, the painter Juan Correa, entitled *Nuestra Señora de los Dolores*, Our Lady of Sorrows. He knelt down, then lay flat on his stomach, on his horse blanket, extending his arms in the form of a cross. His forehead almost touched the painting. It was comfortable that way. His lower back and posterior were sore from the long horseback rides of the past few weeks. Dogs barked in the distance, and then silence took over the night.

A sound, so faint he did not know if it was a breeze coming through the open door or a distant footstep, drew his attention. He turned toward the door just in time to see, in the dim starlight filtering through the opening, a shape disappear outside. It had been in the room with him. Somebody had been spying on him. He got up as fast as his sore muscles allowed and stepped outside. Nobody around. Orion was just slightly east of zenith. Clouds were drifting in from the south. He heard the cry of an elf owl. He stepped back inside, a tingling descending his spine into his legs.

He must be more careful—install a latch on the door. The

man could easily have slit his throat while he was lying flat on the floor, meditating. The Pimas were friendly, but some important people had been conspicuously absent from the welcoming ceremonies earlier that day. Most disappointing was the absence of Chief Coxi. Without his approval the welcome meant nothing. Now he was being watched.... Kino sat down on the floor and waited for his heartbeat to quiet down. Inside and outside there was nothing but silence.

Far to the northwest of the city of Mexico, on the edge of the uncharted world, in the Sonora country at Cosari, this March 13th 1687, he could trust only the celestial favor that transplanted him there. Even the silence was not restful. There was danger in it. It was filled with uncertainty. Was it an opening toward his deepest desires, or the end of the road for a failed missionary? Nothing had worked as he hoped. He had been ready to go to the Orient, to walk in the footsteps of his hero, Saint Francis Xavier. He had been sent to Mexico instead. After three years of hard work on the southern tip of the great desert island of California, as progress was slowly being made founding missions, orders came from headquarters in Mexico to abandon everything. What a failure! What a sacrifice to accept it and move on. To accept it as a celestial favor required more faith than he had. It seemed more like a punishment for his pride. He needed to be humiliated to learn how celestial favors work.

It wasn't all negative. He knew celestial favors were extended to him for protection. One such recent favor had been the papers he was carrying in a leather pouch. They were from the Royal Audiencia, the highest court in the land, granting twenty years of protection from forced labor in the mines to new converts in the Pima lands. He had written a letter asking for five years, but by a great celestial favor, he had been given twenty. The dispenser of celestial favors knew better than he what was needed. A real miracle! He had not dared ask for more than five, yet he got twenty. If only he could tell Chief Coxi about that. He felt doors open before him where he did not expect, while others slammed in his face that he expected to be able to open by himself. Celestial favors were unlike any other. With earthly favors he would ask the person who could grant them, and they were answered positively or negatively. It was easy to relate the granting with the asking. He knew a favor was celestial when what he got was so different, so unpredictable, so disconcerting at times, that the only thing he could tell was that someone much wiser than he was the source of it.

When he got the miraculous letters, he'd ridden for fifty-three days, covering fifteen hundred miles, and made it to Conicari. From there he'd gone to Oposura to confer with Father Manuel Gonzalez, Visitor of Sonora, hoping that Father Gonzalez would send him to the Seris on the other side of the sea beyond the California missions. Maybe one day, from there, he could return and continue his failed work at the abandoned missions.

In the course of conversation, Father Gonzalez had announced, "Fifty miles further to the north, beyond Cucurpe, there are rich rewards waiting for us. The Pimas are ready to receive a missionary."

"Yes, Father." Kino had rejoiced, seeing many opportunities for others in these lands to the north. And then...

"Eusebio, would you accept to go there?"

His whole life had passed in front of him at dizzying speed. He'd marveled, despite his reluctance, at the incredible concatenation of events. Any attempt at prediction or planning how to use the celestial favors always failed.

Is this why I was given a twenty year decree of freedom from forced labor for my converts? Was it not for the Seris, but for an unknown people, the Pimas, somewhere beyond the edge of civilization? He had searched for a polite or diplomatic way to refuse the offer. He could see Father Visitor waiting with a smile for his answer. Did he know the sacrifice he was asking? This was a decision for eternity, an act that would mark his destiny. It was the outside reality crashing into his little imaginary world.

His plans evaporated, and he heard himself say,

"Yes."

So here he was, in Cosari. He'd paid for his endurance ride with saddle sores. His body reminded him of every mile. But he had made a commitment for life, and all else now derived from his acceptance.

He lay motionless and let the place give him an imprint of its reality. There was bad blood between Cosari and the tribes to the west, the so-called Sobas. The chief of the Sobas had killed Coxi's predecessor in a fight. There would be trouble ahead. How was he to use the gift of twenty-year long "freedom from exploitation"? So far, few Spaniards were on this frontier, but the creation of a mission would attract them like bees to flowers. Another dose of celestial favors was needed.

He would unpack in the morning and make a temporary chapel to say mass. He decided to name this place Nuestra Señora de los Dolores, after the painting. He would inquire about Chief Coxi, then start his work. Kino felt for his saddle in the dark, found it, and put it at the head of his blanket unrolled on the ground. Touching the painting in the tube, he commended his soul to The Lady of Sorrows, lay his head on his saddle, closed his eyes, and, in a minute, was fast asleep.

From behind the hut, a man's shape appeared for an instant and disappeared in the dark as furtively as he had exited the hut moments before. Above in the sky, Orion was now veiled in clouds.

Two days after his arrival at Cosari, Kino was putting the last touches to his living quarters. He had set up a temporary hut that would serve as his chapel for a few weeks. He was eating breakfast with his two Opata friends, Francisco Cantor, the interpreter, and Pedro, his blind brother. The brothers had worked in Ures, south of the Pima country, with another missionary, Father Roxas. Their command of the Pima language, and their zeal as helpers, was exceptional. They were gathering up the remains of breakfast when a delegation of five Pima warriors, bows and arrows in hand, signifying they were on official business, came and sat down to talk with the missionary and his helpers. Francisco, the interpreter, translated the conversation.

"Chief Coxi wishes to welcome you and discuss many things with the missionary Kino. Please follow us to sit with Chief Coxi."

"It will be a great pleasure to talk to Chief Coxi. I have been anxious to meet him since we arrived here," answered Kino.

"Then come, and we will talk."

The warriors escorted them slowly across the settlement to a large central ramada. Chief Coxi, his confidants, and his two sons were seated. Coxi made a gesture of welcome toward the newcomers and invited them to sit with them. After brief introductions, he started.

"I have seen great benefits from missions established on lands bordering ours, to the south. Those benefits we would welcome. That is why I have asked for a missionary among us here at Cosari. But I also have seen the changes it brings—loss of our lands to Spanish settlers, forced labors in the mines, and allegiance to Spanish governors. That, I do not welcome. Can you prevent that from happening to us?"

"I cannot guarantee freedom from occupation. What I offer

you is a means to remain free…"

"Free? If we are conquered? How is that possible?"

Kino felt a fissure open in front of his feet. One wrong step and he would fall into it. His faith was so weak…. He could not discern the meaning of celestial favors for his own use, and now he had opened a trap right between himself and Chief Coxi. Would Coxi follow him on what he was going to say? Would he understand the mysterious path he called celestial favors?

"God makes his sun rise on evil people as well as on the good ones. He sends rain to water the crops of the unjust and the just. But they do not profit from it equally."

"What's the difference?"

Coxi was following him, but his astute questioning was daunting. Kino wished he had taken a less arduous approach. Too late. He had to keep climbing. He grabbed what came into his mind, not knowing where it would lead.

"It's the ability to choose the good. Those who trust in Providence see all things as coming from there. They give thanks for all things, good and bad. They see bad things as tests to strengthen their resolve and to depend on Providence even more. Good things are celestial favors. But bad things that fortify our resolve are also favors, if we choose to see them in that light. Occupation is bad but it cannot take away your freedom to choose God."

"God loves Pimas as much as he loves Spaniards?"

"You and your people are more important to Him than the whole kingdom of Spain."

"I like that, Eusebio. That's your name, isn't it?"

"Yes, Chief Coxi. That's my name."

"Eusebio, you bring a new way of thinking. Things are changing and we must think differently. Some tribes have opposed your people and some welcomed you. They all have ended the same way, losing their freedom and their identity."

"I am helping you discover your true identity and freedom. What the future brings I don't know. But the truth of who you are I can reveal to you. That's my job."

"Who am I?"

"You are a unique person loved by God. He guides you and your people. He wants to use you to transform the world. But you have to get to know Him."

"How can I know him?"

"He is present in you and you can talk to Him in prayer."

"When I want to talk to him, do I have to lie down on the ground?"

"Not necessarily. You can kneel, or stand, or walk, or ride a horse."

"Why do you lie down, then?"

"I lie down? What do you mean?"

"I saw you lie down on the ground two nights ago in your hut before going to sleep. I was in the dark, watching you. I saw you lie down on the ground, face down. I heard you murmur words, so I knew you were praying to your God. I had never seen a Spaniard humble himself like that. I saw you were not like the rest of them. I decided to let you stay. I thought you might be useful to us."

"It was you then..."

"You saw me?"

"Only a shadow that slid out of the door."

"Your God protected you then, because if you had seen me or walked toward the other huts to get help, I would have slain you right there. But you looked at the sky and went to sleep. That was a good choice. You see, Eusebio, I had doubts about my decision to let you come here. My people's fate is in the balance. How can I trust you? I don't trust foreigners. I saw you lie down immobile, a sign of submission to someone more powerful than you. I saw you and you convinced me that there was something bigger in you than the words others of your kind speak. I saw in you a man like me, asking questions and hesitating with answers. But you had something I didn't have, somebody worth lying down for on the ground, and trust. I envied you. I wanted to know who your master is. Is that possible?"

Kino breathed easier. Another celestial favor! It came just in time. It was not his cleverness. It had been prepared for him using his weakness and fears. It was prepared while he slept.

"That is why I came. To give you what I have, if you want it."

"What do you want in return?"

"I want nothing."

"No giving up land? No working in the mines?"

"No. I have here with me a written guarantee from authorities that govern the lands to the south, where the settlers and soldiers are. It is a solemn promise that for twenty years, no people from your land can be forced to work in the mines."

"And what happens after that?"

"What is more important is what will have been done by then. More exactly, what the celestial favors will have accomplished in us. Twenty years is a great gift from God. He wants to transform your people, and plant the seeds of His kingdom in their hearts as the mesquite and saguaro seed are planted in the soil of your land. There will be a new world after that. If the hearts of the people change, everything is made new."

"What if we fail this transformation?"

"If we attempt to do it by ourselves, we fail. If we are guided by celestial favors, we will not fail."

"How do we begin?"

"With prayer. First prayer, then work. Build, cultivate the land, and raise cattle, plow, plant, and harvest."

"With what do we start?"

"With the gifts that others have given me. I have seed, cattle, tools, and instructors for the faith. All who want to work are welcome. The product of their hands will be theirs to share with the community."

"What if some want to leave after starting to work and decide they do not want to continue?"

"They are free to leave, but what they have received from the community, animals and tools, for example, stay with the community. Their faith, on the other hand, is theirs forever. They take that with them."

Coxi remained silent for a few seconds then stood up. He dispatched his warriors with orders, and they scattered, running throughout the village.

"Eusebio, I will assemble my people and tell them that we will learn from you the way to follow celestial favors. We have much to do, so we will not delay."

Kino remained speechless. It was amazing—he had felt he would fail, and it succeeded almost without him. Was it when he thought he would succeed, then, that he met failure?

In less than half an hour, all residents of Cosari were gathered around Coxi and Kino. Coxi addressed them. "As your leader I have thought long and have made my decision. It is to accept the missionary Eusebio here in our midst. He will teach us the ways of faith. He will instruct us in prayer. We will learn his skills with cattle and cultivation. We are going to follow what he calls celestial favors. That is our best hope of a happy future. We are protected from the soldiers and settlers for twenty years by a decree that Eusebio has here with him. I ask all of you to respect him. Obey him and his instructors. As for me, I will be here with you to learn, to work, to show you the way. Anyone not pleased with this decision can come to me and I will listen to him. Start immediately to work with Eusebio to learn the new way. Let us begin at once. We are a free people and always will be. The God of Eusebio is going to be ours now, and his favors will help us in our work."

Kino asked the people to kneel and blessed them. Then he sent them in the fields to plant the seeds of new life.

The horses smelled the scent of hay and other horses and galloped to the top of the hill, scattering along the way a gaggle of geese. Sleeping dogs jumped up to join the race. Children screamed, women grabbed toddlers and herded them toward the mission church. The three riders reined in their mounts and yelled to the women not to be afraid. "Buenos dias! A wonderful day indeed! Christ is born for us tonight!"

The women looked back and, hesitating, stopped. Two of the riders were from a tribe unknown to them. The last one was a Spaniard, wearing a black robe similar to Kino's. The black robe spoke words in Spanish that one of the other riders translated into Pima.

"Do not be afraid. I am a friend of Padre Kino. We are coming in peace to celebrate the great feast of Christmas with you. Tell Padre his visitors are here."

"God be with you! Welcome to our home! Reverend Juan Maria Salvatierra, I presume?" shouted a voice behind the riders.

The horsemen turned back in their saddle. Three men were behind them. They had run and were breathing fast. Further behind, six more were running, bows and arrows in hand. Padre Salvatierra turned his horse to look at them. At first glance the men looked alike. Shoulder length hair, naked torso, short pants, and sandals. One had lighter hair and was a bit leaner. He stepped forward. "Forgive my casual attire, Your Reverence. I did not expect the Visitor to the Province of Sonora to honor us with his presence so soon. Certainly not on the eve of the Nativity of our Lord. What an honor you are doing us by coming here to celebrate Christmas with us!"

"So you are the great Eusebio Francisco Kino!"

"Not great, Your Reverence. Please excuse my appearance. I just butchered six sheep for the feast tomorrow. Let me get cleaned up and I will receive you with the dignity due your rank."

Kino shouted a few words in Piman. Salvatierra turned around. A dozen more warriors, arrows drawn, were taking him for target. At Kino's command, they lowered their weapons.

"Sorry, Your Reverence, we are on alert here. Apaches attacked a mission a couple days' travel from here and stole horses. Two men and one woman were killed. We want to avoid similar surprises here."

"Excellent idea, Eusebio. Remind me, how long have you been here?"

"Three and a half years, Your Reverence. Please give me a few minutes and I shall be back. The men will offer you some refreshments. Ask them for whatever you need. My two companions here speak Spanish."

Kino disappeared beyond the mission church. Women emerged from huts bringing baskets of fruit and water for the visitors.

Salvatierra walked around the mission. Everything was orderly and extremely simple. Church and houses were built of mud bricks, and the roofs were of ocotillo and saguaro ribs, with a few larger beams made of oak. The architecture was squarish looking, easy to erect, easy to repair, and functional.

Each building had its purpose—housing, storage, tool sheds, meeting rooms for instruction, a small chapel, and a much larger church for mass. Down below, in the valley, were cultivated fields with vegetables in neat rows—corn and squash —separated by lines of fruit trees. In the distance, he could see horses and an amazing quantity of cattle and sheep. The progress made in three years was astonishing. The number of Pimas working quietly around houses and fields indicated a surprising adaptation of the mission residents to this new life style.

Kino appeared, dressed in his Jesuit robe, accompanied by several women bringing strips of grilled sheep meat with flat bread and dipping sauces, and led his guests under a ramada to enjoy the food.

"Some delicacies for Your Reverence ..."

"Thank you, Eusebio. Do me a favor, let's drop the titles and the formalities. Just call me Juan; I am here as your friend."

"Thank you, Juan. Would you accept to be the main celebrant at mass tonight? The whole village will be here and they would be delighted."

"I would love to do that. But please, Eusebio, you give the sermon. My command of Pima leaves a lot to be desired."

"Certainly! I'll do my best. I'm not completely fluent either. Once in a while, I say something that makes them laugh. Some expressions I haven't yet mastered."

"I was admiring your mission, Eusebio. You chose the site well, and the houses are solidly built. The fields of vegetables, the trees, and crops are well tended. It's a marvelous sight. Well done!"

"Thank you, Juan. The people are eager to help. They do everything with devotion and joy. They learn fast and improve on the techniques. I just show the way and they take over."

"How many parishioners do you have?"

"We had more than three thousand baptisms, but parishioners come from long distances and move about with the seasons. We are fortunate to count among the baptized Chief Coxi, his wife, and two sons. He helped bring other dignitaries from settlements to the west and north into the fold."

Juan explained why his visit was scheduled so soon after the foundation of Mission Dolores. The Jesuit Provincial for New Spain was under pressure to justify sending missionaries to regions so far north where, according to rumors, there were no souls to be saved except a few heathen tribes. Others were saying that the northern frontier led to great nations and immense mineral riches.

"I was sent here, Eusebio, to bring back the truth and squelch rumors."

"Come and see the truth as it is, with your own eyes. I will take you to see the missions at San Ignacio, San Jose de los Imuris, and Remedios. You can write your report from what your eyes have seen."

"Eusebio, you read my mind! You're a man of action and few words. I can hardly wait to get started."

They became friends immediately. Juan inquired about the difficulties Eusebio had encountered. He told him about the opposition from shamans who spread lies, saying the missionaries hanged uncooperative Pimas or poisoned them using evil oils on their foreheads. In one village, Spanish settlers had come and tried to force Pimas to work in silver mines. When they refused, the settlers called for the cavalry. They came and hanged some Pimas, giving the shamans more substance to spin their stories around. But no dust-throwing shaman could stop Kino from coming and refuting their fables.

"What gives you courage to continue, alone and so far from

civilization?" asked Juan.

"It's not courage. It's a continuous supply of celestial favors that keep me going. Nothing happens the way I want. Experience taught me that I have to surrender all my plans. When the Apaches raided the neighboring mission, I took five warriors and spare horses and went to investigate. We organized watches and prepared to defend the mission. Five nights later, the thieves came back again. This time, they were met with armed resistance and fled. Fifteen warriors jumped on their horses at daybreak and took after them. I joined them to prevent a war, if I could. A couple of miles from the mission, my horse pulled up lame, and I had to lead it back, limping. The others caught up with the Apaches. They had camped and were resting. It was a massacre. Only two Apaches escaped. The others were scalped, and our party came back with more horses than had been stolen. But more importantly, five women who had been kidnaped from another Pima village nearby were freed. As a result, they asked me to baptize the whole village. Until then, they had refused to hear about conversion. You see, even raiding parties are used as celestial favors to make things happen the way God wants it."

"I admire you, Eusebio. You can see good coming out of difficult events. You may need this gift in the future. There are many who would like to close your missions here. They say that they are too remote, that we should consolidate, not expand. Some want to call the Jesuits to become teachers at universities..."

Kino registered the blow and paled slightly for a few seconds.

Then he said, "Even if the seed must die first, it is to produce a great harvest. Some plant, some harvest, some are called to die. I will concentrate on celestial favors and not worry about the results."

Children led the procession that evening, with Father Salvatierra following them, wearing a special white and gold silk chasuble expertly sown by artistic hands in Mexico City. Padre Kino was next, in a more modest cotton chasuble made locally by Pima hands, but no less resplendent of white and gold color, with stars embroidered on the edges and a cross with red cactus flowers on the center. Chief Coxi and his retinue walked nobly behind, carrying lit candles. An impressive choir, with men's and women's voices, sang Christmas hymns in Pima and Latin. The mission church overflowed with the faithful crowding every door and spilling outside. And celestial favors fell like starlight on all present.

Chapter 3

The message was scribbled on a brown paper bag: "You stole our merchandise. Return it within a day or you're dead. At the intersection before San Miguel by the picnic table you'll find a note in the garbage can. Follow the directions."

Manuel put the brown bag on the kitchen table and looked at his nephew Rodrigo. "That's all? How did you get this?"

"It was against my door this morning with a rock in it," he sighed. "What do we do?"

"You move in with me, here."

"And then, what?"

"You're safe here. We can see anything coming miles away. Anybody that comes knows that he is being watched. No surprises here."

"Let's do what it says…"

"They'll kill you for sure. They'll have you where they want. No. That's dumb."

"What else can we do?"

"Wait for a celestial favor."

"Maybe you wait for whatever. I can't afford the luxury."

"You need it more than me. It's you they're after."

"Where's my stuff, Tio?"

"It's not yours—as your friends just reminded you. If I tell you, you'll want to return it. Right now, it's a stalemate. They need their merchandise, you need time to figure out what to do. You stay here, where it's difficult to dislodge you. The police are watching this place. That makes it risky for your friends to harm you while you're here."

Reluctantly, Rodrigo moved in with him. The deadline came and went. Nothing happened. Silence.

Manuel's urgent problem became how to civilize his nephew. Rodrigo was a wild mustang, but Manuel was determined to tame him. He was afraid to ride him too hard; the young man might just bolt and run.

At least he should domesticate him enough so he could sleep peacefully at night, unlike last night. He'd heard Rodrigo tossing and sighing for hours. Manuel, unable to sleep also, went outside to watch the stars, as was his habit. At dawn, Rodrigo joined him there and they sat in silence. After a while they came in to make some coffee. Manuel started a pot boiling, fried some eggs and toasted bread. They ate, lost in their own thoughts.

"Hey, sobrino," Manuel broke the silence, "help me do the dishes."

Rodrigo slowly emerged from his reverie and dumped his breakfast utensils in the plastic dishpan filled with warm water. He could not hold back a deep sigh. Manuel urged him on, saying, "Stop worrying! You're safe, nothing can happen to you here. Make yourself rare until things settle down. We'll figure out what to do next."

Rodrigo looked into the graying light announcing the sunrise. The valley was still dark, as daylight crept over the mountain top and extended fingers down the slope, toward the bajada below the house. Saguaro shapes emerged from the shadows.

"Tio, tell me what you did with my stuff. I'll be able to protect myself. I'm a sitting duck here. I got to move."

"The less you know, the less you can screw things up, that's my opinion. If anybody asks, you don't know. Truth is your best helper, Ruy. When it's time, I'll tell you."

"When is it going to be time?"

"As soon as we get a celestial favor that tells us so."

"What crazy favor you keep talking about?"

"It's something that happens to you to make you take action."

"Something already happened to me, and I have to take action fast. Let's not wait."

"We don't know what to do. We didn't get any clue yet."

"Whose crazy idea is this? Where did you hear about such nonsense?"

"I learned it from Padre Kino."

"Who's that?"

"You should know, Rodrigo."

"Oh, the guy that founded the mission? He's been dead for centuries! What would he know about my problem today? Things are completely different now."

"Some things never change. How to read the signs of the times, how to make sense of an event, so that all things that happen to you happen for your good."

"What happened to me happened to try to kill me."

"You're still alive, and it happened to make you change for your good."

"Just tell me where you hid the stuff and let me do the rest. Who made you my guardian angel?"

"You did! I fled to this desert to avoid problems like this. You came to me and I gave you my word. Now we're in this together."

"You can't hide it forever! You can't keep it, and you can't get rid of it. They'll find it and we'll find ourselves in the pen in Yuma."

"You underestimate your old tio, muchacho. I told you. Nobody can find it, no matter how hard they try."

"Everybody knows it's somewhere here. The police suspect it, and that message..."

"If anything, it proves that whoever threatened you has no clue about what happened to the stuff. As long as they don't, they need you alive to find it."

"How long do you think I can stand it? I'm a prisoner here."

Rodrigo walked to the door as if to run away. He stepped outside. Down in the valley he saw a car slow down near the road to their house. Maybe the police. He came back.

"Hey! Come on, Rodrigo. You're free to go. But use your brain. Stay here as long as you have to. If you leave, somebody will find your body in a ditch."

"Everything was going great! I was making money. They told me I would have to take two hundred kilos, twice the normal weight, just this once, to prove I could handle it. And what happens? I'm caught in a death trap."

"Listen to me. This is your chance to get out of that trap. You're going to change your life and you're going to do it clean."

"And do what? Tell me what I do if I give this up? You got a job for me?"

"I have something better. Here's a chance to start over. Face the truth. You can correct your situation."

"Truth? Nobody knows the truth. It's everybody for himself and may the best win."

"Yeah! Who's the best?"

"The smartest, the one with the most money."

"Money means smart to you?"

"Truth, you can't count—money, you can, and you get what you want."

"That kind of smart will get you out of this trap?"

"Maybe! I don't know! I'm ready to blow up!"

"Listen! When I'm in trouble, I ask myself why I turn around in circles, like a vulture. Those birds circle around until they find dead deer. You too have to find what can feed you. And it's not carrion. Look for the food that's meant for you."

"And you, you know what food you're looking for?"

"It's celestial favors you and I need. We need to learn from experts... someone like Kino, a real expert."

"He's not coming back from the dead to teach you!"

"There are many ways to learn. Wisdom is built into the world. Ask for wisdom. Learn to look, to see, to listen. Stars can speak to you. Stop gliding through life like a bird that eats dead food. Find out what your heart is looking for. Now is the time. You don't sleep. Listen to the wisdom of your own body. Will you trust me?"

"I'm stuck with you."

"I want more. I don't want to have to drag you behind me. I want you to choose to come with me."

"Where?"

"Wherever I take you. Deal?"

"Bueno, deal! But how long?"

"As long as it takes."

"I hope it doesn't take too long. That's all I can say."

It didn't take long at all. The next day, immediately after Manuel left for Sells to buy some groceries, Cesar and Paulo, as if they had been waiting for that occasion, drove up to interrogate Rodrigo. They were friendly, encouraging Rodrigo to open up to them. Not at all the attitude they'd had when, at his house, they'd demanded to know where he had dumped his merchandise. Cesar was especially tempting. "Don't get me wrong, Ruy, I know how difficult it is to get a job these days. If I was your age, I probably would do the same thing you did. Believe me, it's not you we want. Not even Sureño. He just gives you your merchandise. We want the ones who're in charge of this business."

Rodrigo could barely refrain from shaking. They knew who gave him the drugs... who else did they know about? Del Norte, who got them from him? They probably knew more than he did. Might as well tell them everything and get it over with.... But he didn't know where Manuel had hidden the stash. And this phony, sugary friendliness! They called him Ruy, like his grandma used to. He was confused. Nothing was clear. Everything was a trap. He kept his eyes on the ground, and it seemed to wobble. Did it wobble because he was confused? Did the earth care? Would anything on earth stir if he dropped dead? Did Manuel love him? All seemed lost, so he grabbed on to his promise to Manuel.

"You can trust us, Ruy," Cesar cajoled, "We're not against you. We just can't let two hundred kilos of merchandise circulate freely around here. It is our interest... I mean our job, to get it back in a safe place. That's all we want."

Rodrigo glanced at Paulo, whose eyes were glaring at Cesar, a deep furrow on his forehead indicating his disapproval of what Cesar had said... something about their interest in recovering the merchandise? Why would cops have interest in that? They were not on the level with him. Maybe they knew more than they pretended. The silent disagreement reinforced his uneasiness.

"I don't know where it is. That's the truth," he said.

"Then tell us who you gave it to," encouraged Cesar.

Rodrigo remained silent.

"You don't trust us, Ruy," Cesar took over. "Big mistake. Help us now. We get the merchandise off your hands, and you don't worry about it anymore. You refuse, and we focus on you as prime suspect. Don't expect any forgiveness from us then. OK, speak now."

Rodrigo took a look at Paulo again. The cop was composed, waiting for his response. Rodrigo, stubborn, lowered his head.

"Sorry, I know nothing."

Cesar and Paulo looked at each other with a cold stare, got up, neglected to say goodbye, and left.

Chapter 4

A groan of grinding gears signaled that the drive of the Mayall four meter telescope failed to counteract the motion of the earth. The field of view of the instrument drifted away from the dust cloud in Orion on which it had been focused. Hank Wagner suppressed a profanity, shut down the drive, and closed the dome. He called in the anomaly to maintenance and verified proper storage of his night's worth of observations in the central data warehouse.

Not quite four in the morning—almost time for the observatory to go to sleep anyway. He decided not to stay on top of the mountain but go back to Tucson.

On the way down from the summit, he rolled down the windows. A gentle breeze flowing from the top of Kitt Peak carried a cold scent of pine and juniper. Above him, on the heights, the telescopes closed their Cyclops eyes one by one as technicians finished check-out routines in anticipation of the next night's observations. Hank drove to the edge of the road, got out of the car, and leaned against the door. The faint glow of the approaching dawn on the other side of the mountain did not yet penetrate the western horizon. Orion hovered over the distant Ajo Mountains. Through his binoculars, the great M42 nebula in Orion's sword was visible, hanging from the belt of the hunter.

The long night-hours spent counting photons streaming in from this nursery of new stars and taking wide-field images were going to pay off. Those far recesses of the universe were organizing, condensing from dark matter, producing light and releasing energy. He felt lucky to be able to do some observing, now that he had taken on a duty as administrator. He felt responsible for the welfare of the observatory and its workers. Mishaps like the one tonight were to be eliminated. What had happened to him should not happen to others. He would have to find a way to do maintenance *before* things broke. The competition for observing time was fierce, and trying to extract more money from government agencies was almost impossible. Hank was the soul of the observatory. He had to keep the instruments humming and the astronomers happy. He had to think of them first, even at the cost of giving up his own investigations. His new duties were added work but, surprisingly, quite satisfying. He'd had to make a quick transformation from investigator preoccupied with his own research to a sort of guardian angel for this whole community whose main purpose was to spy on deep space from the summit of Kitt Peak. It turned out to be soothing for him. His new duties allowed him to take a more global view, to consider the whole community of observers. There was an ebb and flow movement in it that affected his outlook on life. He had to give momentum to the ideas of others, help obtain grants and contracts, and watch from the sidelines as others reaped the benefits of the seeds he had sown. Unexpectedly, it added strength to his confidence. It was like a melody with a constantly changing rhythm, with sudden crescendos, soft peaks and gently trickling decrescendos. His own research was more a frenetic, obsessive beat to observe, analyze, and publish before anyone else had similar ideas.

During the longest nights of the year, Orion struts across

the sky, showing off his imposing shape, once dead but now enshrined in the heavens. Stereotype of the hero, he wants to maintain his standing by shrewdly using his relationships. Hank had spent a good part of his career studying the constellation of the hero Orion, son of Neptune, killed by a scorpion's bite to the heel. Diana, goddess of the hunt, pleaded with other gods to give him an imposing place in the winter night sky, safely removed from the constellation Scorpio.

Until recently, Hank was convinced he only needed his intellect to stay away from scorpion bites. To free oneself from destiny, or bad genes, one has to continue the struggle for liberation with the help of science. We are positioned halfway between inanimate objects, like the boulders above the road, and pure intellects, unimpeded by material state, that analyze, classify, and create virtual objects to discover the truth as revealed by mathematics. Astronomy, among all sciences, is best suited to discover mankind's origin and destiny, which is written in the stars. It has the past and the future in front of its instruments. Our intellect travels back to the genesis of time and looks into the future by simply observing in different parts of the universe.

Now he felt a desire for looking at life differently. He viewed life not as being driven by the necessity imposed by random events, like gears seizing in a drive, for example. Instead, he saw life as a mysterious rhythm that carries us, as in a piece of music, toward a carefully prepared finale. Events, then, have a meaning, they contain information that prepare us for that final end. Nothing is cheap, nothing nonsensical, or irrelevant. Everything is part of a larger context, a piece of the puzzle that makes life adventuresome.

If only his family life could be understood in such context. There, chaos and futility reigned. He was helpless in the wake of his wife's sudden departure, taking their daughter with her.

He had not seen them in months. That event remained, for him, impossible to decipher.

Down in the valley on the west side of Kitt Peak, toward the village of Sells, a few lights could be seen, dimmer than stars. His attention was attracted by a flicker of light down in the valley, near where, he guessed, was the main road through the Tohono O'odham reservation. The air was so clear that the slightest spark was visible. Down there lurked challenges of a different sort. A steady stream of people ran day and night through the nets set up by federal and local police trying to intercept illegal immigrants sneaking into the country. The Tohono O'odham border with Mexico was a desert mostly without roads. Was there meaning in those events also?

Suddenly, a stone rolled down the slope on the other side of the road. A grunt and a stampede of hooves on asphalt shattered the silence. The car jerked with a bang, and he opened the door to take refuge inside. A band of javelinas passed, then silence regained possession of the night. He ventured cautiously to the other side of the car. A hubcap, slightly dented, lay behind the front tire. He threw it on the front seat and jumped behind the wheel.

In the valley a few miles further down, he stopped, unlocked the gate protecting the astronomers' world from unwanted visitors, and locked it behind him. As he was getting back to the car, he had an uneasy feeling that he was being watched. He looked across the road. A man was standing there. Then he caught sight of the semi-automatic rifle, like an AR-15, that the man was pointing at him. It had a huge magazine, with more than a hundred cartridges. The man stood there, holding his weapon, looking at him.

Behind him, he now could see a group of about fifteen men and women, most of them carrying backpacks, with plastic bottles of water hanging from belts, immobile as statues. They seemed indifferent to what could happen to him. For them, the intrusion he represented was not their concern; they had more important worries. It was to the man with the gun to decide.

The man motioned him to come closer. Hank took ten of the hardest steps of his life and stopped. The man took a pack of cigarettes from his pocket and offered him a smoke. Hank, unable to speak, refused it by a small gesture of the hand. The man lifted his index finger to his eye then to the sky and said, "Telescopio?" Hank understood immediately.

"Yes, I work with telescopes on top of the mountain."

The proximity of the road, and maybe the potential danger that noise of a summary execution could represent for the little group by revealing their position, made the coyote choose mercifulness. The man smiled, put a finger across his lips to indicate Hank should be silent, and with a swift gesture indicated he should go. Hank did not wait for explanations and departed in a shower of gravel from the tires.

He started breathing normally again as he saw the first houses near Robles Junction. He eased off the accelerator as the images of the coyote and his group faded from his mind, and he slowly rejoined the world of the city heedless of what was happening around it.

Hank took River Road and then turned onto Camino Kino. He could see, spread out at his feet to the south, the city still asleep in subdued lights. He pulled into the driveway, parked his car and entered the house. He tiptoed toward the bedroom where he could distinguish a form in the dark. She was sleeping.

He continued to the kitchen, filled a glass with cold water and sipped it in silence. He was lucky to have found Pilar. She worked as a real estate agent in Tucson. Her relatives lived in Phoenix. After his painful separation from his wife, Kim, and his daughter, Celine, he'd sold his house and hired Maria Del Pilar to help him find a new one. After several weeks of looking at residences, none of which seemed to suit, they'd started to look at each other more than at houses, finding each other's company more exciting than house hunting. So they'd rented this place near the Catalina foothills, temporarily available, with a lease renewable every year for as long as the owner decided to stay in Australia. That was convenient. He would have time to finalize his marital situation and then decide on buying a house, and maybe a life with Pilar.

Life was short, and the incident this morning made him realize it could be shorter than he estimated. He would talk to Pilar and make a fast decision. Why wait?

He walked to the bedroom, his pulse rising rapidly with desire, anticipating her smell and her embrace. He got out of his clothes rapidly and slid under the covers and extended his arm to touch her. He got an unpleasant shock when his fingers reached not the warm, soft body of his companion but a cold pile of pillows. He rolled to turn on the light. At the head of the bed, on another pillow, he saw an envelope with his name written on it. He tore it open.

> Sorry to disappoint you, Hank. Please forgive me. I have to get my head straight and understand where our relationship is really leading us. After five months together, I have learned to love your presence, your voice. But what is the future for us? I know you will never give up your little Celine. How are we to build a future on such shaky foundations? I know I will never be able to have you completely. There will always be obstacles. It is better if I give you up. It is because I love you, believe me. I'm going to Phoenix for a few days. I need to do this for myself, for both of us. I'll call you

when I figure out a few things.

Love you,
Pilar

Hank stuffed the letter back in the envelope then flipped it across the room. It bounced off the wall hard and flew out in the hallway.

Nothing in his private life worked! Nothing lasted. Nothing flowed. A constant staccato of uncertainties. She could have given him a warning, had a conversation. Instead, the pillows, this ridiculous letter.... That's the amount of trust she had in him?

What irked him most was that Pilar had used some of the same words his estranged wife Kim had used. Kim was an excellent homemaker and a devoted mother. Hank had thought they had a great relationship. Kim was the life of parties at the University, at professional meetings, at business occasions. So many times Hank's fellow astronomers had remarked that Kim was the perfect astronomer's wife, never complaining about long nights when he was gone, weeks when he was on travel in foreign countries. They were beatifically happy, weren't they?

Then, slowly, Hank started to pick up a tone of complaint when Kim confided in him. She would say that she was not the ultimate object of Hank's love. He protested that he was the most faithful of husbands, and she agreed. What was missing was her place in the orderly design of Hank's life. She said their life was a succession of unconnected moments, some pleasant, some meaningless, going nowhere. She accused him of being able to understand the working of dark globules of prime matter in Orion better than what was at work in the recesses of her heart. Hank had to admit she was right. She had recognized the secret of his passion for science. He could get lost in his work. He could quiet his fears and uncertainties by plunging into the stream of successes or disappointments of his research. Lately, he found solace in the rhythm of working for the survival of the place he administered. There was continuity of flow there. It carried him toward an unknown goal. Abandoning himself to the flow brought more satisfaction than even personal glory.

What he had prepared himself to be was a scientist. He had not spent any time figuring out who he was supposed to be for others or even for himself. Kim and Celine were for him sources of pride, but otherwise a mystery. He had been a provider of material security and comfort, a place of safety in a material world. He had given them everything but himself. There was a chasm between his life as a scientist and the rest of his life. But what was the rest supposed to be? Kim was asking him to be somebody he could not even imagine. He wanted Kim to trust him and let him be himself. What he loved in her was what he was not. He did not want her to read him like an open book. What he enjoyed in her was the mystery she was.

Inexorably, the downward spiral continued until Kim finished him off with a line of reasoning similar to the one that Pilar had used. "I have made up my mind, Hank. You, belong to the world of international science. My love for you has to be sacrificed. I give you your freedom back. I am leaving you. True love has to renounce the joys attached to the possession of its object. Goodbye Hank, let's stay friends."

There was something wrong with this reasoning, but he could not figure out what it was. He told her she was hasty and would regret it. She answered with a great abundance of tears. And Hank, ever since, had tried to expel from his memory the agonizing scene of Celine being taken away by Kim, screaming, "Daddy! Daddy, I love you! Come with us!" Even now, almost two years later, remembering that made him a bit nauseous. He jumped up from the bed, steadying himself against the door jamb until the floor stopped spinning. He felt cold, grabbed his robe in the closet, and tightened the belt around his waist to warm up.

Back in the kitchen he downed the half-empty glass of water, then poured himself a small snifter glass of expensive tequila. He sat down in the living room and watched the dawn sky spill over the range of the Catalinas and snuff out the lights of Tucson. If love is reasonable, then why have two women I loved declared that true love never reaches its object? If love is a chain of successes and disappointments that we follow to forget the past and the future, then its end is futility. But if it is a river that carries us to a real destination, then it must reach its object. It is not only the beginnings that are pleasant, the end must be its true fulfillment. In any case, what is needed is perseverance, and patience in order to reach the end, not flight and abandonment.

Was there any meaning in what happened earlier this morning? Or was it a return to staccato-living—random events with no connections? Which one?

He walked into his study and looked at the mail piled up on his desk. Six articles ready for his final approval before publication. One was from his nemesis, Andre Gautier, who was almost always opposed to his theories.

He spilled a few drops of tequila on the bill for rent of his residence.

Impossible to sleep. The events of the morning kept him wired. By instinct, he took refuge in his work. A coworker had sent him the name of a man who specialized in preventive maintenance. Maybe he could hire him to set up a program to schedule early maintenance for the most heavily used telescopes, to eliminate forced idleness due to breakage of essential parts, like gears. He sat down with his laptop and wrote a proposal to use discretionary funds to start a six months trial to prove the feasibility and accuracy of such predictions. He selected the name that was suggested to him. Roger La Torre came highly recommended by his former employers. He was a specialist in the field, a man who had practiced diagnostic and prediction of maintenance for many years with a good reputation for success. He finished his writing and emailed it to the members of the steering committee for review and approval.

The sun now shone over the Catalina Mountains. He went back into the living room, threw himself on the sofa, and fell into the arms of Morpheus.

A couple of days later, Hank was returning home when, from a distance, he saw Pilar's car in the driveway. The trunk was open and half-filled with clothes. He parked behind her car and saw that she had piled boxes and suitcases in the entranceway to the house. She came out carrying a picture frame to add to the pile. "Hi, Hank! I have come to get a few of my things. I am moving out. I will get the rest of my stuff later." Hank looked a bit crestfallen. "What's going on? Are you leaving?"

"I made up my mind, that's what. I spent the past week reflecting, and I decided it's not right for the two of us to play make-believe."

"And what are you going to do?"

"Move in with Greta for a while until I find a new place."

"Greta convinced you to do this?"

"She didn't know a thing. I asked her to let me stay with her."

"Then who talked you into doing this?"

"I made up my mind while talking to a nun." Hank raised his eyes upward, looking at the sky in dismay. "You talk to nuns now? Where do you find people like that around here?"

"I went to see them at this monastery near Phoenix on the advice of my Aunt Rita. She knew them and arranged for me to drive there and talk to one of them."

"So you took the advice of an old hag in medieval clothes, and of course she told you to leave me."

"Hank, you are ridiculous! She is about my age. She is the happiest person I have seen in years. We didn't talk about you at all."

"Then what did you talk about?"

Pilar pointed an accusing finger toward him. "You believe you are the only subject I can talk about? We talked about what love is."

"That's a good one! You who want to stop loving me, and this nun who never knew what it is to love?"

"She knows more about love than you and I together."

"Fine! OK, tell me!"

"Hank! Be fair now. I'm still trying to learn this. I'm just able to sort out a few ideas. But it was what I needed to hear."

Hank sat down in the trunk of her car. "Let's hear it. Maybe that's what I need too."

"Good! I always believed that love was unattainable. We can grab small morsels, but it escapes us like a dream we don't exactly remember. What's real, I thought, is the enjoyment of the moment. And then it disappears. With you, because of Kim and Celine, not even those moments were real. It was all futility."

She looked at Hank, waiting. He sat upright in the trunk, his chin on his fists, eyes lowered. She hesitated and continued. "What I discovered talking to this nun, is that love is not unattainable, that there is no stopping short of possessing it. Real love is a continuous desire for attaining the object of our love, interspersed with moments of joy when we are touched by the presence of this object and the hope to possess it one day."

Hank leaned forward as if to get up but decided not to interrupt her. What she was saying was amazingly close to his own recently acquired conviction. Any events, or moments, not connected and flowing toward a goal were futile. This nun in the monastery may be on to something.... But what was that end?

"You know, Pilar, you can have all of me right now."

"But Hank, it's not you I hope for."

"Is there someone else?"

"You can be one who leads me towards attaining love, but you are not my ultimate goal."

"Oh boy! If you compare me with God, I'm out of the picture!"

"I don't compare you, Hank. You can be an instrument to help me get there, and maybe I can be the same to you, but man and wife, we cannot be. You already gave yourself, Hank, and you cannot take it back."

"Why not? It didn't work. She left me. Maybe with you, it might work."

"It won't, Hank. It didn't work because you and Kim didn't give it your all. Once you give your all, what else is left?"

"You don't even want to try?"

"Try futility? It cannot work."

She was right, he knew it. He was not the end she was searching for. But then, what was the purpose of meeting her? Another unconnected, incoherent event...He could not abandon himself to a flow that went nowhere. Everything in his private life was senseless.

"There was a purpose in my meeting you, Hank. It was an invitation to act as two mature persons, out of love for all involved. Don't get me wrong, Hank. You will always be for me the first dim light signifying the dawn. You put me on this way."

She must be reading my mind, he thought. He felt defeated and just wanted out of everything—the relationship, the conversation.

"Me? Please don't blame me for that."

"Without you I would never have thought about eternal light-years of creation, new stars forming from the dust of dead stars. I hope I can bring you something to make you stop and change direction."

"Talk about it! You are destroying what we were trying to build together."

"Hank! What you and I shared was not love. It was human desire for fulfillment masking the source itself of fulfillment."

"Call it what you want, I was happy with it."

"Happy with a sham? Didn't you desire the truth?"

"What is truth? For me, science is truth. I have no time to ask who I am, or where I am headed, in hope of a distant future."

"You're using your work as a drug, to deaden your desire for truth."

"Maybe, but it's bearable."

"Hank, you scare me. Wake up before it's too late, before you ruin your life."

"Pilar, let it be. You have made your choice. I made mine. I've been happy, or at least I thought I was happy. But I've not yet been zapped by the light of a monastery."

"Hank, I hope you get zapped very soon."

"I will call you then, Pilar. Let's stay friends. Take your time moving out. No hurry."

They got close and hugged like friends. Pilar loaded her car. Hank moved his car out of the way. She left without looking back, her cheeks wet with tears.

Hank went inside, limping, as if a scorpion bite had paralyzed his heel.

Chapter 5

Kino's caravan was the only thing moving in the desert for miles around. The mules and horses were walking fast. They knew they were going home and they hurried. Their load was light, now that the sacks of food and seeds and gifts had been left behind. They'd passed El Comac and were cutting south toward the San Ignacio River.

Nobody ventured in this uncharted territory belonging to the Soba tribe with impunity. The Soba owned the lands to the west, around Caborca. Their elusive chief was known only as Chief Soba. He asserted he represented his people, and no other name was needed. Reported to be everywhere, he was seen nowhere. His commands were on everybody's lips, but no foreigner had met him in years.

Recently, Kino had received some indications that the elusive chief was inclined to talk to him. Vague enticements in the form of gifts of mysterious sea shells, the likes of which he had never seen, were brought to him. He suspected the shells came from the Pacific coast of California, yet the gift bearers affirmed they were not brought by boat from there but came from lands to the northwest. He waited for a more official invitation from Chief Soba, but it never came.

Kino firmly believed that all events have meaning and bring information that should be interpreted as celestial favors. After waiting for years to find an opening toward the western tribes, he construed the sea shells and the reports of the chief's intentions as signs that he should make a foray into the forbidden land and bring the benefits of his mission to the Sobas. Lieutenant Juan Matheo Mange, at the head of a section of twelve cavalry men, was giving escort. Kino at first refused the escort, but the Lieutenant was the nephew of General Jironza, and refusing was not diplomatic. In the caravan was also Chief Coxi, the leader of the tribe with whom Kino had established his first mission, with a retinue of sixteen warriors.

For over fifteen years, the two tribes had coexisted in a state of deep distrust. Coxi had facilitated Kino's work and reaped the benefits of the decree from Mexico that Kino had obtained, protecting the tribe from encroachments by Spanish settlers for twenty years. Chief Soba had offended Coxi's tribe when, trying to prevent the establishment of a mission there, he'd killed Coxi's predecessor.

Kino was puzzled. He hoped the time for reconciliation had come, and he had brought gifts. At Caborca they were welcomed by a crowd, including children, holding arches of flowers for them to pass under. The villagers were excited by the arrival of the caravan. Residents avoided the cavalrymen and Chief Coxi, but surrounded Kino and his mule train. The missionary distributed his gifts with instructions on what to do with seeds and tools, and advice on how to care for the domestic fowl and fatten them before eating them. Kino searched the surging crowd anxiously, looking for somebody who could be Chief Soba by the entourage that surround chiefs when they appear in an official role, but there was nothing of the sort to be seen.

Two days passed, and still no sign of Chief Soba. Manje and Kino decided to push further northwest, all the way to the sea. After an arduous advance in a harsh desert, they arrived at the

Sea of Cortez. They climbed to the top of a mountain, and with the help of a spyglass they could make out land to the west: California. Looking far to the north, they saw the end of a gulf and more land. California was not an island! Not equipped for a long expedition, they returned to Caborca. Manje was now impatient to go back to his uncle, the general, and announce the great discovery. For him, that eclipsed everything else he could possibly see in the land of the Sobas. Kino had to slow him down. There was missionary work to be done.

He called the village together, made them sit down, and instructed them. "We are to love our enemies, even those who have harmed us or killed our relatives. Chief Coxi is here to show that he wants peace with you here at Caborca. He has no desire for revenge. He wants peace with the Sobas."

That created quite a stir, and for a while part of the audience looked around as if to find a missing actor in the drama. Kino sensed it was Chief Soba they sought. Then, as if on command, all heads turned back to Kino. The missionary seized the occasion. Maybe Chief Soba was there, if not, certainly they would report his words. He told them that all events have to be seen as celestial favors, sent to influence our conduct. Good things, like the gifts he had brought, were signs of God's favor. But even bad things, like the murder of Chief Coxi's predecessor, were not signs of celestial disfavor. They were not obstacles to make us turn aside. They were tests to make us choose how we interpret them. "It is the choice of our conscience that counts," he insisted. "The future is not determined by evil and murder, but by our choice."

"Choose the good, never evil." The challenge was to change evil into good. The murder had created rancor and animosity for all these years. The choice now was to see the murder as an event allowed by Providence, a potential celestial favor if they continued to trust in its benevolence. It was not a permanent diversion from good but a test of faith in Providence.

"If we can see individual events as tests and choose to continue trusting, the effect of evil will disappear. Our individual consciences become the soul of the whole tribe. We pass from difficult obstacle to celestial favor. The two tribes can be united again."

They all listened, waiting for something or someone, but nothing happened. Chief Soba was less in evidence than signs of vegetation covering his desert land.

The brittlebush had lost its cover of yellow flowers, ready to endure the dry weeks until the start of the monsoon season. Ocotillos had dropped their leaves, waiting for rainy days. The air over the gently rolling land shimmered as the sun climbed higher in the sky. The celestial favor bestowed on them to safely come into the land of the Sobas and return unharmed seemed to have been otherwise unproductive. There would be no new mission there.

One of Coxi's men, riding ahead of the group, turned back toward his chief and extended his arm toward what appeared to be a column of smoke, or a thin vertical cloud on the horizon. Chief Coxi raised his right hand to acknowledge his man and signaled him to continue ahead. Antonio, who was following Coxi's group and Manje's point man, picked up the hand signals and saw the smoke also. He turned his horse around and galloped to Manje's side to report the sighting. Manje gazed at it. It was dissipating already, a wispy cloud of dust, hardly visible anymore. "Probably a dust devil, Antonio. Don't worry about it. Go ask Chief Coxi what he thinks of it, if you want."

Antonio galloped back to Chief Coxi's side. "Lieutenant Manje said it was a dust devil that we saw. What do you say?" Coxi smiled at the man and gestured toward the path straight ahead. Antonio dropped back to his assigned position. Coxi gave a short order to his men to look out and be ready for combat. Horses picked up the smell of water, still a couple of miles away, and accelerated the pace.

Manje was satisfied with the trip. He had counted every Pima he saw, written down their numbers, and taken notes on the lay of the land. But that was nothing compared to what they had discovered. There was land to the northwest connecting Pimeria and California. Expansion to California was possible by land.

His report about the trip was all written in his mind. It was going to be very optimistic. This was a great new land for the Kingdom of Spain, and his uncle, General Jironza, and even the Viceroy in Mexico would be pleased with his accomplishments.

He congratulated himself that teaming with the Jesuit Kino had been a great move. When Kino was around, the natives seemed more at ease, less fearful. He had gone with other expeditions on military raids against horse thieves. The Pimas usually were tight lipped, declining to say anything but "Pima"—We don't know. When they saw cavalry, most of them took refuge in thickets of cholla, or disappeared into the hills. Most of the time, he and his men ended up talking to old warriors past their prime and toothless grandmothers. Not on this trip! He had met some very lovely Pima señoritas this time.

He remembered with pleasure the young women he'd surprised on his way to the sea. They were filling water jars, some made of pottery and some of woven fiber, using ollas they dipped in a pond of fresh water. And they were mostly naked. At first they'd run away. He'd pursued them and convinced them to come back. They giggled and laughed for several minutes before they picked up the jars and walked gracefully away. That had been a most memorable encounter. Maybe Pimas could be tamed, instead of scared into the hills.

Manje looked ahead and saw Coxi and his group descending the last escarpment toward the river. Manje's point man was about two hundred yards ahead of the second group and a good half mile behind Coxi.

Kino rode beside Manje, recalling the events of the last few days. Over all, the results had been mixed. The Sobas were a bit more reserved than the Pimas back near Dolores, but well disposed toward them. There was, however, disappointment. Chief Soba remained invisible. Were the invitations inaccurate? And the sea shells? Did he come in vain? Was there to be no mission in Caborca?

Chief Coxi and his men were down in the riverbed, watering their horses. Manje's point man suddenly raised his hand and yelled to stop. A short distance ahead of him, forty Sobas had seemingly materialized out of the ground. Manje spurred his horse and galloped to investigate, with Kino right behind. In the group were also women, mostly very young, except for one, more mature, who seemed to be in charge. One of the men came toward Manje and bowed to him. Manje asked him who he was.

"I am Chief of the Soba people. I have come to salute you and to talk with Padre Kino."

Manje was surprised. This man looked like the others, nothing distinguished him as a chief. "I salute you, Chief Soba! It is a great pleasure to see you face to face. It is indeed an honor."

Without a word, Chief Soba bowed again and walked toward Kino, who was dismounting his horse. Manje could hardly keep from laughing. So this was the great Chief Soba about whom people talked with reverence! The man was unarmed and wearing only a very brief loin cloth and sandals. The women were flimsily clad, wearing rabbit fur below the navel, the rest of their body uncovered. Some carried on their heads beautifully woven baskets made of grass, containing food and water. Manje dismounted also and walked toward the señoritas to look them over at closer range.

Chief Soba made a discrete sign and the women walked away slowly, followed by Manje and the rest of the party, leaving Kino with him. Manje ordered that a few bags of piñoles be distributed to the women. After a short hesitation, the women accepted the piñoles and put them in their baskets. Manje and his friends were now even closer to the women, who kept on walking until Kino and Soba were at a respectable distance and could speak without being overheard.

"Kino, your friend the young soldier is a fool. Beware of fools of any age. We heard of his interest in our young women at the pond by the seashore, the other day, and we figured he would be easy to distract. I came to talk to you privately. The women are here to draw him away."

"Chief Soba, I have been waiting to meet you. Finally, we see each other!"

"Kino, I saw you years ago. I saw you before you arrived at Cosari. I was informed you were coming and followed you before you reached town."

"Why did I not meet you then?"

"It was not time. I came with a club to use on your head if I had to. I was not sure. I figured that Coxi might do it. Better him than me, since you were going to his town."

"So why talk to me now?"

"I got to know you well since I first saw you. I have thirty warriors on each side of your caravan, as an escort, to make sure your cavalrymen and Chief Coxi leave my territory without incident. I killed Coxi's uncle, and I could have killed him too for coming into my lands without asking me. He owes his life to you. Keep him away."

"He owes his life to me?"

"I'm not ready for peace with him. Had he come without

you, he'd now be dead. He says he wants peace, but nothing's changed between us since he became chief. I'm responsible to my people for the decisions I make. Changes are coming, and we have to deal with them. Understanding the changes in the midst of the lies that gush out from the mouths of both the civilian and military authorities invading our land is impossible. They promise protection from the Apaches, who never come this far west. Who needs such protection? But we are asked to obey a power that does not respect our traditions."

"Nothing will change between your tribes or with the Spaniards until you change."

"Me, change? Why me?"

"You killed his uncle. You started the war. You have to change evil into good first."

"That's what you said in Caborca... I didn't understand."

"You were there? You heard me?"

"I'm everywhere my people need me."

"Evil is what you did. It blocks the future. Evil cannot determine the future but it prevents good from working effectively. You cannot change what you did but you can change its effect by changing your heart. Then things can flow again and the future can be shaped without obstacles. You are best qualified to make it happen."

"But I hate my enemies. How can I change that?"

"Become a little bit like a child. You have to see as a child. See all things as coming from a loving Providence. Then things can flow again, freed from the past. If you change, you can become the conscience of your tribe, and they'll follow you."

"I have to see that happen. If I see it work, I'll believe it."

"You can see it if you want. I could start a mission in Caborca. You'll see it then."

"For seven years now, you have prevented Coxi's people

from being enslaved. Would you do that for us also?"

"Yes. The protection would be extended to your tribe. But that's not a good reason to start a mission."

"I could see the change work. Teach me how. You said we have to be like children. I want to see that! Come as children, you and your friends. I will make a pact with you. Send me children to work among us and I will help you. We will welcome you with arches of flowers carried by children. But the moment you act like masters, the pact is broken. Do you accept?"

"You want me to send children? Where am I to find such men?"

"If you cannot find them, come yourself. Is it impossible to find others like you?"

"I am not able to choose the men sent here. It's a miracle to get even a few. If you want to be picky, it complicates matters."

"What's so difficult? Ask what you called Providence. Ask! We can wait. "

"All right, I'll ask Providence to send missionaries who are children."

"Then, Kino, bring your Providence, and teach us how to see. Build a mission in Caborca," Chief Soba extended his hands to rest on the shoulders of a dumbfounded Kino. "Always let my people know you are coming. Send messengers. Let me know. This is a desert land, but not a land without a people."

"But you're so hard to find, Chief Soba!"

"I'm not. Not to you from now on. Send for me from anywhere, and I'll come immediately. But beware of your friend Manje. He's full of ambition and will step on your head in order to rise higher. When he's with you, he's acceptable to me. Do not send him alone. Look at him now, he's looking for trouble, he's getting too close to my wife!"

"Your wife?"

"Yes, he's talking to my wife. She's my advisor. She's the one who suggested that we welcome you with children and flowery arches. She can read men's minds and she has figured out your friend Manje. Give me your word that you will not reveal what we talked about. Not to Manje, and not to Coxi. Tell them we agreed on a mission for Caborca, but no more."

"If you insist. Why the secret?"

"Let fools think that I am a fool. Idle words can ruin the best laid plans."

Manje and his entourage came back laughing. "Chief Soba, your ladies are all very gracious!"

Chief Soba bowed again to Manje, and remained silent. Then, turning to Kino, "It was a pleasure to talk with you, friend. We shall talk again soon."

"With the help of Providence, it will surely happen."

As abruptly as they had come, the forty natives climbed a small ridge and vanished. Kino looked toward the river. Coxi and his men were cooling their feet in the wet sand of the stream. Chief Soba's protective escort of warriors was nowhere to be seen.

Manje gave his impression of Chief Soba to Kino. "Hard to believe he is a Chief. I have never seen a more unimpressive figure among the Pimas. He travels unarmed. He must be so poor he can't afford weapons any more than he can afford clothes. You seem to have become friends. What did you talk about?"

"He wants a mission at Caborca."

"Are you going to build him one?"

"If we find the right man to take care of it."

"You didn't waste time, my friend. I can't say the same thing. Those women were a bunch of cackling quails."

"Let's join up with Coxi. Let's stay together."

"Why? In the land of Chief Soba, we come and go as we wish."

"I wouldn't push our luck that far, Matheo."

Manje ordered a halt to let the horses drink in the pools of water left in the bed of the arroyo. Coxi came nonchalantly to talk to Kino.

"How was your talk with Chief Soba? I was wondering how long he was going to wait to come and talk to you."

"You knew he was coming?"

"That was no dust devil, back a while ago. Smoke, in the desert, means somebody is coming. I guessed it was Chief Soba and his warriors."

"You were right. He wants a mission in Caborca."

"Good! That means we can have peace."

"Let's pray for peace, Chief Coxi."

After a brief pause in the arroyo, they left and reached Magdalena in the evening, and the next day they arrived back at Dolores.

Chapter 6

"Padre Kino, there is a runner here from Caborca, and he wants to see you immediately."

"I'll talk to him right away."

Caborca! It may be Saeta's response to his invitation to spend some time here. But why send a runner instead of a letter by ordinary carrier? Good news seldom travels by runner. He hurried in the courtyard. As soon as he saw him, he knew something was wrong. The man was exhausted and his face was anxious and grim.

"What news do you have, son?"

"Very bad news! Padre Saeta is dead!"

Kino looked down at the ground to make sure it was not opening to swallow him up.

"How did it happen?"

"Warriors from Tubutama came and demanded to talk to him. After a few words, they shot him through with arrows. He died on his bed clutching a crucifix. By the time we realized what happened, the murderers had gone. I ran as fast as I could."

"Does Chief Soba know this?"

"He must know by now. Runners were sent to him even

before they sent me to you."

Kino felt the weight of a sinful world press on his shoulders. He staggered back into the chapel to unburden his aching heart. "My God, forgive me, I have sinned. I sent a child into this wilderness. I should have gone myself and let him get more experience right here at Dolores. He was my special child sent to the Sobas, and they loved him. Now we will have merciless punishment from the Flying Cavalry. They always punish the innocent first. Was it my will and not yours that he should go to Caborca? Let me bear this suffering for those who murdered him."

He felt a bitter disappointment, almost despair, envelop him. He looked at the altar and he saw the cross. "My God, why have you abandoned me? Do not punish them for what they have done. It's time for mercy! Have mercy on my child who died in your service. I should have died there, not him. How do we continue now? What should I do to pay the ransom for the guilty ones without bringing down the whole work of salvation in Caborca?"

His eyes burned and his vision blurred. A stream of tears flowed along his nose, down his sunburned cheeks, and dropped onto the rough black cloth of his robe. Failure again in the midst of victory, as in California. Was he doomed to repeat his failures? There it had been the order of the King that severed the first bloom of success; now it was his trust in Chief Soba and his own sending of this missionary-child that was to shut down all chance of progress. It is not easy to trust in Providence! This really is Good Friday. Saeta's death made the cross a bit too real. Why him and not me? he wondered. He was Saeta's leader. They killed the wrong man. They should have shot me full of arrows. He looked at the cross again. He was wrong. He was not the leader. The leader was on the cross. Now he was there too, except he was not dead. He suffered for the whole community, for himself, for the Pimas who loved him, those who hated him, the Spanish settlers, the Flying Cavalry whose fury was about to be unleashed against the Pimas. This was the ultimate test. How could good come from this devastating event?

It had been very difficult getting Saeta assigned to Pimeria. There was always strong pressure to keep missionaries from this region where mines were being developed at an accelerated pace by the Spanish settlers. Missionaries were troublesome. New missions meant new areas where Pimas could not be exploited for twenty years. Kino had to use very delicate diplomacy to have a new man assigned. He sent Saeta to Caborca because his youth, dedication, humility, and enthusiasm were really childlike. He gave Saeta an excellent start with cattle, sheep, trees, and seeds, and the ranch in Caborca was prospering as a result. The Sobas were enthusiastic about it. With support from Chief Soba, Caborca could become another anchor of the missionary chain, like Dolores. Not like the missions at Tubutama and Remedios, where peace was always fragile. News of discontent and insubordination had arrived from Tubutama. Residents there disliked that they had to take orders from Opata Indians employed by Father Janusque. It was a delicate situation. The Pimas there were not yet ready to take over, and the presence of the Opatas was necessary, at least for a while longer.

He would talk to Janusque about that. The sooner he resolved that irritation, the better. Maybe the mission at San Xavier del Bac, to the north, could one day become a strong foundation. Then he could move there and let somebody else take over at Dolores. The further away from interference by military and civilian authorities the better. He should go far away to forget the disgrace of this failure. Send us a child, the Sobas said. Now the child had been sacrificed. What good could come from this disaster?

A shadow briefly darkened the light pouring in through the door. He looked up and saw Luis, one of his Pima aides, waiting for him outside.

"Yes, Luis, what do you want?"

"A muleteer just came from Caborca with a letter for you. Here it is."

Kino quickly opened the letter. It was from Saeta! He quickly read it and pressed his fists against his eyes, groping for understanding. Saeta had written the letter a short time before he was murdered. The muleteer was evidently passed over by the runner and got here after him. He was writing Kino that he was going to stay at Caborca for Easter and thanked him for all his help. The fields were rich with harvest and he had many children to care for. They attended mass every morning, and catechism twice a day. They were preparing for First Holy Communion, and many adults would be baptized at Easter. He had scribbled two messages after the letter. One said he had heard of troubles in Tubutama where two Indian helpers had been killed. The other, on the outside of the envelope, was asking for prayers and instructions on what to do. Saeta had a forewarning of trouble, and stayed anyway.

Saeta's death was devastating for the missions, and an enormous challenge for Kino's faith in celestial favors. He saw it first as a punishment. Was he trusting Chief Soba too much? Was the chief more interested in protecting his people for twenty years than seeing them convert and trust in Providence? Punishment by the Flying Cavalry would hit the Sobas and those in Tubutama as a whirlwind of sabers hacking and lances piercing. Did he bring that too on them? All things work for the good of those who love God. How could good come from this? Had he, in his folly, prevented Providence from acting, by creating an impossible situation?

A gulf of despair, wider than the Sea of Cortez, was opening in front of him, He remembered a similar situation he had experienced when he was a student in Austria, preparing to take his first Jesuit vows. He fell very ill and everybody expected him to die. He was given the last rites. In a moment of reprieve from illness, he prayed to Francisco Xavier that he would intercede for him. If he could obtain for him just a few years to become a missionary to the Orient, he would be happy to give his life for all the people in India, China, and Japan, who needed missionaries so badly. A few hours later, the fever left him, and in a few days, he was back in school studying. Ever since that day, his health had been flawless, and his endurance legendary. But he never went to the Orient.

Now in a chapel on the edge of the known world, the apostle of the Pimas asked for guidance from his patron saint again. At that time too, he thought it was an end, but it was, instead, a new beginning. Yet nothing ever happens the way we imagine.

Saeta was gone. Kino could not imagine what was to become of his missions. Yet slowly the despair subsided and a desire for action took root in him. The next day, he wrote a letter to General Jironza, offering to go investigate the cause of the murder. He begged him not to make rash judgments that would compromise the work so beautifully started by Saeta. He gave the letter to his most dependable Pima rider with the fastest horse. "Go quickly and come back immediately with an answer."

It took three weeks before Kino began to see improvements. Jironza had agreed that only the murderers would be punished. The Pimas had agreed to turn them in. Those not directly involved in the murder would be spared. It was agreed that the murderers would be turned over to the military at the village of El Tupo. Maybe peace could be maintained after all. He gave thanks to God and prepared to retire for the night. It was getting dark outside, and the entire mission was silent. As he finished his night prayers and was about to lie down to sleep, he heard a soft rattling noise against the door. He got up to investigate, when a half-naked man stepped in, with both hands extended in a sign of peace.

"Kino! It's me, Soba. Don't get excited."

"Chief Soba, you are like the wind. You come and go unannounced."

"You live longer that way," said Soba. "Kino, I must talk to you. I can't go on like this anymore."

"What ails you?"

"My sins, that's what."

"Since when are you burdened by sins, Chief Soba?"

"Since my son, Saeta, was murdered, and I couldn't prevent it. I had given my word to you. Send me a child, I said, and I would welcome him among us. He was a son to me. I loved him, and my people loved him. And then some hot heads from Tubutama—my own flesh and blood—come, pretending to be friends, and murder him out of hatred. I sent men to find out who they were, intending to put an end to their miserable lives. When I heard who they were, my heart broke in pieces. I know them all. They wanted to help the people, to correct injustice in Tubutama, they said. One of them is from Caborca. He killed Saeta, not because he hated him, but because some hotheads told him that all changes in our customs are causing injustice. He would have killed you too. I asked him why he didn't kill me, after all, I was the one who asked you to send us Saeta, who was to me like a son. He came to his senses then. This man has been unable to sleep ever since. He says the spirit of Saeta haunts him, and he cannot bear it. He is ready to die. He said he wants to turn himself in to the Cavalry."

"Let's talk about that later. What about your sins, Soba?"

"Oh, it's driving me mad! Saeta was a child, innocent, and trusting. Why was it he who got killed? Why not your friend Janusque in Tubutama? He's older and he's not like a child."

"Maybe that's why Saeta was chosen, because he was innocent as a child."

"You said that nothing happens without Providence. Was Providence asleep that day?"

Kino looked at Soba suspiciously. Did he come to tempt him to despair? He had barely been able to answer that question to himself. Now Soba reopened that painful wound.

"Providence is not protection from injury or death. It is a grace. It is like a seed. It is not for the consumption of the sower. It brings fruit after it dies in good soil. The better the soil, the more abundant the harvest. It is because Saeta was a more fruitful candidate to receive grace that he was elected. His murderers thought they were in control. But their victim was not random, he was chosen."

"But now our child-missionary is no more. Who's going to take his place?"

"Another will be called, who will hear the call and respond to it."

"Who is that going to be? You said it's hard to find good men."

"It is hard. But I'm not the one choosing—God is. He will send the right person to do the work."

"What do I do? My shoulders bear the anxieties of my people. Now we have this new danger. Everybody is talking about fleeing to safer places for fear of the Cavalry. They look at me as their leader and I feel I'm the guilty one. I got them into this mess."

"Maybe you should confess your sins and receive absolution."

"What does that do?"

"It makes you a new man, and it gives you a new task."

"A new task? Which one?"

"That's up to Providence. If you want to be useful to your people, that's the best way to do it."

"Then I want to confess."

"You have to be baptized first. You have to join the Church family."

"I want to join."

Kino put his sandals on, found a candle, and they entered the mission chapel. He stepped into the sacristy, put on his liturgical vestments, took a small flask of holy oil and a small cup of water that had been prepared for the next day's mass, and led Soba to the chapel. He lit the Easter candle, and started giving instructions to Soba about what he was going to do.

"Usually I pour a lot more water than this on the adults, but since you want to be a child, this small amount of water will do. What name do you want for baptism?"

"What name?"

"You have to choose a saint's name."

"Saint Saeta!"

"Not so fast," laughed Kino. "He's not a recognized saint yet."

"That's the name I want. I want it to be like my son's—Saeta."

"Take his first name then: Francisco Xavier."

"All right, then! That's what I want: Francisco Xavier."

A shadow standing in the doorway between the sacristy and the chapel stepped into the dim light of the candle.

"Ah, Luis! I was looking for a godfather for Chief Soba. Maybe you can be the one. Would you accept?"

"Me? For Chief Soba?"

"No way!" shouted a strong voice.

Five warriors stepped in front of Luis, led by Chief Coxi. "Is my friend the great Chief Soba hiding from me? Why do you come in the dark like a coyote?"

Kino stepped forward, "Chief Coxi, this is a great honor for your village. Chief Soba wants to be baptized, right here in your village, in this chapel."

"That's what I overheard. And that's why I said 'No' to Luis. A chief needs another chief for godfather. I would like to be his godfather, if he accepts."

Chief Soba was so surprised he stood speechless for a few seconds.

"Well? What do you say?" asked Kino.

"It would be a wonderful thing," answered Chief Soba.

They proceeded to the back of the chapel and Soba knelt down. Kino poured the renewing water over his head. When it was over, Coxi seized Soba's arm to help him up and they embraced.

"Now we're brothers, Chief Soba."

"Yes, we are brothers, Godfather Coxi."

Soba followed Coxi out and they went to the ramada to talk under the starlit sky. Kino stayed in front of the crucifix.

"Your ways are mysterious, O Lord. Lead us into your peace."

A month later, in early June, Kino rode to a place called La Cienega, near the settlement of El Tupo, outside the village of San Ignacio. It was a place of springs, where cattle were herded and people could meet in open surroundings. La Cienega was outside both San Ignacio and El Tupo, on open land. It was neutral territory, amenable to holding discussions between Pimas and the troops of General Jironza, which would congregate there. Kino was there to give confidence to the Pimas that it was not a trap. The murder of young Saeta was far from forgotten. Kino had extracted from Captain Almazan, local enforcer of the law in the region, a promise that peace and pardon would be extended to those who had not participated directly in the crime, and to those who were willing to deliver the murderers to the authorities. Delegations had been sent to Tubutama to encourage Pimas to turn in the perpetrators. They were supposed to come to La Cienega. It seemed like a favorable turn of events.

But then Jironza's troops went to Caborca and burnt all the fields of wheat so carefully cultivated by Saeta and his faithful. Kino vehemently complained and irritated some officers when he declared, "It takes the brain of a burro to think that burning the wheat fields of my poor Saeta would punish the local Pimas. They did not organize the attack, and they were on the side of Saeta. You are punishing yourselves by this act. What is needed now are pacifying words to get the Pimas on our side." The military, after mulling it over, reprimanded the troops. But the civilian authorities disagreed, and recommended severe punishment to set an example. So the troops had gone to Tubutama, applying strong-arm methods and profuse threats. This only made the Pimas very suspicious. So Kino was dispatched in order to repeat the promise made by the military that they would be well treated if they obeyed the directives. Kino camped at La Cienega with five helpers from Dolores, waiting for the events to unfold, praying that the fragile understanding would last and that the troops would not do anything rash.

Before sunset, as Kino was reading his breviary, a half-naked familiar shape appeared next to him. "Is that you, Chief

Soba? What brings you to this place?”

"Zeal for the welfare of my people.”

"Are you not afraid to be surrounded by troops and recognized?”

"That's a risk I take. Kino, I have come to warn you. You're being betrayed by your own kind. Beware of infiltrators, those who come talking peace while in their hearts they hide plans for murder.”

"What are you saying, Chief?”

"There is no intention to keep peace here. They lied to you. They have told you to convince my kin to come here in peace. I know you believe that. But that's not what's going to happen. I know for a fact that Captain Solis, not Almazan, is on his way here. My men are watching his march here. He'll be here tomorrow.”

"Solis? Impossible! It's Almazan and some of Jironza's men.”

"It's Solis, the butcher of Pimas. His presence spells disaster for you and for my people. Kino, watch out! You're surrounded by traitors. Not only on the military, but also on the Pima side. The governor of Dolores, Tubic, that snake, who came to round up Pimas in Tubutama, he's a traitor. He doesn't have love in his heart. He treated those accused of helping Saeta's murderers worse than the soldiers did. He hates me too.”

"Why would he hate you? There's peace between your people and Coxi's people.”

"Obviously, you don't know. He is the son of El Podenco, former chief of the Pimas in Dolores, whom I killed. Coxi forgave me, but that snake, Tubic, never did. He has infiltrated your men to pursue his own plans. He's not clean, he's a deceiver. And he wants revenge for his father's death. I know that for sure. Kino, listen to me. Most of the people around us here do not want to resolve this situation peacefully. They want vengeance. Depart from them! They will destroy your reputation."

"My reputation is not important. Nobody knows who's an infiltrator for sure. As for separating the good from the bad, it's not for us to do. The military wants to separate good Pimas from bad Pimas and rid the world of the bad ones. Who are they to judge who is guilty or innocent? And if the guilty want to make amends, somebody has to be there to show them the way."

"If you stay, you might be killed!"

"The only way to deal with evil is to turn it into good. That's the way of the cross."

"So we do nothing and stay here, like rabbits, so the coyote can catch us?"

"No! We do something very powerful. Providence has a plan for this particular situation. We stay so that evil cannot conquer. We are celestial favors in the midst of danger. It takes more courage to stay."

"What gives you courage, Kino?"

"Grace."

"Where can I find grace?"

"In confession and communion."

"Then give me this grace right now."

Kino and Soba huddled, kneeling on the ground in the darkening light. Chief Soba confessed. Kino made the sign of the cross over his bent forehead, and then Chief Soba remained silently kneeling for a moment. Kino removed from around his neck a tiny pyx he carried under his large pectoral cross. He fumbled a while, trying to open it with his rough fingers. Finally he succeeded and removed a fragment of consecrated host. Soba received the body of the Lamb of God, and remained kneeling for a long time in the dark, as the stars started to sparkle above them.

Early next morning, Solis, at the head of his cavalry, marched in and established camp on the edge of La Cienega. Soon after, he visited the camp of the Pimas who had come from Tubutama. They had been there for three days already, waiting for him. They had come, bringing the accused murderers, humble but confident, expecting pardon. Solis separated the accused murderers from their companions. The accused ones were kept under armed surveillance and the soldiers built a thick circular wall of cholla cactus five feet high. This caused great distress among the companions of the accused. They expected punishment for them, but not humiliation. Then Solis called a meeting with the Pima leaders, and demanded that the accomplices of the murderers and the ring leaders be brought in to watch the punishment. This now created a bigger stir. It was not what had been decided. How would one know for sure who was an accomplice anyway? It would require more time, more roundups of people. Solis said he had time and would wait. The governor of Dolores, the son of slain Chief El Podenco, Tubic, that snake, as Chief Soba called him, was chosen to lead the roundups and decide who was an accomplice.

Three days later, a group of fifty Pimas came. Before reaching the camps at La Cienega, they left their weapons at the edge of a grove of mesquite trees. Among them was the son of Chief Soba. The unarmed group was led to the clearing by the springs, where the rest of the Pimas were waiting. Now the mounted soldiers formed a circle around the Pimas who were gathered in the middle, like cattle to be sorted for branding. Soldiers on foot, with unsheathed sabers and lances, were preparing for the punishment. Solis was in the midst of them. Then the Pimas who had been in charge of the latest roundup started pointing out the accomplices. As they pointed out the men, soldiers on foot in the circle started to tie them up. This created an uproar and the horses became skittish, some rearing up nervously. Suddenly, a Pima ran to the perimeter of the circle of excited horses and, escaping the attention of the mounted soldiers busy trying to stay on their mounts, slipped inside to join those surrounded. Tubic suddenly pointed at Soba's son. "This man is a murderer, and the son of a murderer!"

A soldier grabbed Soba's son and attempted to tie him up. But the Pima who had slipped in grabbed the soldier and threw him to the ground yelling, "Live, my son! Through the grace of God! Live!"

Solis took two steps and swung his sword with all his might. The sword came down with a heavy "whoosh" on the neck of Chief Soba, severing the head, and it fell onto the ground. Pandemonium erupted, and it became a violent free-for-all, soldiers and cavalry swinging at Pimas, and Pimas running for their lives. When it was over, forty-eight Pimas, guilty and innocent, had been killed. Tubic looked over all the bodies and identified Chief Soba among them. But Soba's son was not among the dead.

The aftermath was a disaster for the missions. Burning and pillaging continued for months. Only those missions directly under Kino's supervision were spared. The military and civil authorities praised Kino for his magic touch with the Pimas, thinking it was his personal initiative that prevented the burning of his foundations. Kino somberly denied it, but to no avail. His friend Manje later described proudly, in one of his memoirs, how, in one instance, he alone stayed with Kino and hid the chalices and sacred vessels in a cave, anticipating the firestorm. What Manje did not know was that very night, after he had barricaded himself in his room, Kino was still praying in the open chapel, and there, in the dark, a figure stepped up to Kino's kneeling form and said, "Have no fear, Kino. I am Chief Soba's son. I am in charge of the rebellion. As long as I live, I will keep your missions untouched. My father gave his life so I could live. I know it was your influence that made him do that. My father loved you. Maybe after this wind of folly is over, you can teach me what you have taught my father. I want to know what he knew. I want to have his courage. Maybe you can tell me the meaning of the word 'Grace' he pronounced before his death. That must be a powerful word."

Kino turned around to face the voice. The man was gone.

Chapter 7

Manuel parked in front of the administration building, on top of Kitt Peak, grabbed his report and walked in. Hank met him in the hallway.

"Hi, Manuel! You got the final report and the bill?"

"Hi Hank. Yep! I got both. We have work to do. The electric power lines will have to be cleared in some places from the vegetation growth underneath. And your water ponds need enlarging. You need more water for the fire trucks, or you might lose a few buildings. Another fire like we had last summer... you can't count on the wind changing direction again."

"OK, we'll take a look at your proposal. Come into my office." They sat down in Hank's small office, crammed with books, reports stacked on the floor, and with barely enough room for two computers.

"How are things with you, Manuel? I haven't seen you in a while."

"Can't say it's all great. My nephew moved in with me. I'm trying to get used to it."

"Your nephew? Didn't know you had one."

"We've never been close before. He got a death threat so I told him to move in with me."

"Death threat? That's serious! What happened?"

"Oh... it has to do with illegal immigrants bringing in drugs. Somebody accused him of stealing and threatened him if he didn't return what he stole."

"You think he stole drugs?"

"No! I know he didn't. But that won't put an end to the threat."

"These are crazy times. This business of drugs and immigration is out of control. The other day, I was going home early in the morning, and I got stopped by an armed man leading about a dozen immigrants with backpacks—probably drugs. The coyote could have killed me. I lucked out; he asked me if I worked at the observatory. When I said I did, he let me go. That was scary. I could be dead."

"Where did it happen? Near here?"

"Down at the gate, near the main road. I stopped to lock the gate, and this armed man was there."

"Did you tell anybody? The police?"

"No. I have more pressing problems right now. This seemed to be a fluke. Scary, but temporary. My other problems are longer lasting..."

"Worse than being killed?"

"Not sure. I have to get used to living by myself. My wife and my daughter left me."

"Sorry to hear that, Hank. Maybe I'll send you my nephew, Rodrigo. He's quite entertaining," chuckled Manuel, trying to cheer up Hank.

"Thanks, Manuel," smiled Hank. "I wouldn't be a good companion to anybody, these days. Did you tell the police about the threats on your nephew?"

"No. I'm like you, Hank, except I like to live alone."

"It's not good for man to live alone, you know, Manuel."

"I lived alone until now. I could choose the good things and avoid the bad ones as I wished. I could string together a long list of good ones only. It was good music, steady and soft. Since Rodrigo moved in—on my suggestion—his bad things are mine too. Now it's like waves—three bad ones, one good one...I lost the rhythm. Nothing holds together. Too much dissonance, everything is disconnected. The good is submerged under the onslaught of the bad. I need a conductor. I need to get the rhythm back."

"I know what you mean. I'm submerged too. When I have to fight for the survival of the observatory, I find that soothing. The rest sounds like cacophony, not music. Can't make sense of it. You and I need to join a choir and try to sing together. It may help."

"My choir so far sounds like a pack of coyotes howling. Your suggestion might be good. Except... we need to find a choirmaster."

"It's a deal, we'll look for one." Hank glanced at his watch. "Right now, though, I must get ready for another meeting. Do me a favor, bring your proposal and bill to the finance department, at the other end of the building. Explain to them what you want and let them take a look at it."

"Sure, Hank, I'll go right now."

Hank studied Roger La Torre sitting across his desk. The need for a reliable technique to avoid downtime was paramount. Roger had come up to the observatory on top of Iolkam Duag Mountain, otherwise known as Kitt Peak, to finalize the details of the work. Hank had taken him to see the telescopes and explained the process for starting his work and getting paid.

Of medium height, whitish hair, sparkling blue eyes behind rimless glasses, he wore a deep blue shirt open at the collar, khaki pants and comfortable walking shoes. In his late fifties or early sixties, Hank figured. Roger had worked for aerospace companies on the west coast and Phoenix. He'd started his consulting company in Tucson a few years ago.

"So we'll be able to predict the failure of a gear before it happens?" asked Hank.

"I believe so. We have to test them thoroughly. That will allow us to detect and read the events that signal the onset of deterioration. If we read them correctly, we will be able to predict when they are not reliable anymore."

"That information is in the events?"

"Yes. The gears have a potential well, a zone where they are reliable, and are meant to be used in that zone. When they get less reliable, they signal, by small deviations from that zone, that they may pop out of the bottom of that well and enter a zone where they deteriorate rapidly. The trick is to represent that safe zone, at the bottom of the well, with accuracy, using specially designed tests."

"That's how you read the events?"

"Testing and statistics give us a picture of the zone where the gear is safe, and when it starts to move out of the zone. When they do, it's time to repair."

"It would be nice if we could get that kind of picture for events in our life, so we could react to them in time," mused Hank.

Roger glanced quizzically at Hank. He seemed serious, not bantering.

"Human events cannot be analyzed that way. Too many components enter the picture. Mechanical events have much fewer degrees of freedom."

"Can you still say that events in our lives carry some information?"

"I believe so. All events bring us information. We can't read them the way we read gears because those events are not repeatable. The statistics are not clear."

"Then... how can we read them?"

"We have to trust that they bring us something for our good."

"Trust? Even negative, painful events?"

Roger was tempted to avoid answering directly. They were deviating from talk about the failures of gears. Was Hank testing him? He seemed genuinely interested, though. He might have his reason for asking. So he ventured further.

"Negative events are our tests to see if we will stay safely in our potential well or if we decide to jump out of it. Gears don't decide—the stress environment does that for them. For us, it's different. We make the decisions."

"And what is our potential well?"

"It's our zone of comfort, where we find fulfillment. Good things we take for granted, as if they were due to us, and we don't care where they come from. Bad things we complain about, and blame Providence, or luck. They force us to make a choice. If we decide that they're due to random luck, there's no meaning in them. We might as well move to a place where we can avoid such things. If we believe that all things are celestial favors, and that good can come from them, then yes, they have meaning. We trust that they happened to bring us help in the future."

Hank picked up a pen as if to write something, then put it down. There was a suggestion that might quiet the cacophony in his life. Good music required staying in what Roger called our potential well. But transforming bad events, like his broken relationships with Kim and Pilar, into celestial favors, that required something more: trust. And trust, well, he couldn't do that.

"Where did you get the idea that bad things can become celestial favors?"

"It's not an idea, it's a fact. Nothing is random, everything is planned. I couldn't believe it myself until I learned it from Padre Kino, reading his biography and writings. For him, everything was a celestial favor."

"You mean the Kino who founded missions around here?"

"That's the one. He said everything, pleasant or unpleasant, has a purpose. We don't see it, we can't figure it out, but it's meant to lead us to fulfillment by choosing the right path, the path of faith in Providence."

There was a gentle knock on the door, and before Hank could say anything, it opened slowly, with hesitation. "Come in!" snapped Hank, somewhat abruptly.

Roger watched as a big hulk of a man walked in. Gray strands of hair on the temples contrasted with jet black hair on top of the head drawn back in a ponytail. Jean jacket over a pale blue T-shirt, with matching jeans covering well-worn pointed-toe cowboy boots. He carefully closed the door behind him, bending his frame slightly to say hello to Roger. He walked with assured steps toward Hank.

"Excuse me, Hank. The finance guys need your signature on the proposal. They say you have a meeting in five minutes."

"Yes, Manuel, thanks. I'll sign it as soon as I get there."

Hank got up, and turned toward Roger.

"Manuel, this is Roger. He is going to work for us and help us maintain the telescopes. You probably will run into him around here over the next few months." He started to walk out, then stopped. "Manuel, you're the one who told me about Padre Kino?"

"Sure... why?"

"Roger, here, and you have something in common. You're

both experts on Kino. Ask him about that. And you want to consider him for your choir also. Ask him about that too. Well, I must go to that meeting. See you, Manuel! See you, Roger! Roger, you can start anytime. And some day you must tell me more about your potential well and celestial favors." Hank left.

Manuel and Roger walked out together. Manuel, at six feet four inches, looked like a giant saguaro above Roger who, closer to five feet ten, stood as a staghorn cholla next to him. They glanced at each other, with a bit of reserve. Manuel broke the silence.

"Buenos dias. I'm Manuel, Tohono O'odham Electric Utility. I work with Hank. I bring power to his telescopes."

"Roger La Torre, self-employed engineer." They shook hands.

"I come here often to see Hank," continued Manuel. "He is overworked. Ever since they gave him this administrative position he is hard to pin down for anything. He refuses to give up his research. Now he is up night and day. He is going to have to shed some leaves like an ocotillo in dry season, if he wants to survive."

"I'll be working for Hank to try to keep his telescopes from breaking down when they are not supposed to. Hank was interested in my philosophy of life, it seems."

"Oh yeah. He often asks me about my vision of life. My vision is obscured by dust storms lately. Hank thinks that my Tohono O'odham heritage gives me some wisdom that modern men have lost. He doesn't realize how thoroughly modernized and consumerized we have become. We had more wisdom before. Our own wisdom, and wisdom borrowed from the old folks that gave us a better vision, like the Jesuit Kino, for example. Hank said you know about him?"

"I read his biography. There is a big heavy book published many years ago that's still the best, better than those new ones you can buy now.”

“Yes, I know that book. It reads like a novel. I read it as a kid. I wish I could find it and read it again.”

“I have it. If you want, I’ll bring it to you.”

“Really? That would be wonderful! How come you have that book? What got you interested in Kino?”

“We have a few things in common, I suppose. He wanted to go to China, he was sent to Mexico. He wanted to convert Baja California, he converted Pimeria. That reminds me of perturbations in my plans I experienced in my life. He helped me see that events in our lives are all ‘favores celestiales’ as he called them.”

Manuel took a deep breath and slowly pressed his left hand over his pony tail to smooth some invisible waves. “You believe in that too? I thought I was the only one—with Kino, of course— who believed the same.”

“He’s the one who convinced me, reading his life and what happened to him. Even bad things are there to help us and keep us on the right path.”

“I read that too. But I think he also said that this needs faith, and needs support—support from others who believe the same thing. A kind of choir. If you sing by yourself, you need an extraordinary voice. But in a choir, others help you, they support your voice. The blending of voices, like in Gregorian chant, makes it magnificent. You cover my weaknesses and I help you reach the higher notes. You agree?”

“You’re right. The union of voices creates a common soul in the choir so that belief flows from one member into another. Kino wrote about that.”

“You’re a rare bird, Roger. Forgive me for saying so. I’ve got to tell you this. Until recently, I lived like a hermit, and I liked it. Then some things happened, and I realized that I needed advice on how to make good things come out of very bad ones. I need other members in the choir, to help me believe that bad things can be transformed into celestial favors. A bit earlier, Hank volunteered to join the choir. Would you be interested too?"

"Why not? How many members do you need?"

"Right now, it's Hank and me. We both experienced some of those favors that require the support of a choir. Come join us. We'll learn to chant. I warn you, I don't know much Latin, so we need a choir director. Maybe you can be choirmaster."

"I'm not sure about that," laughed Roger. "I'm no expert in chant either. The blind leading the blind... you know the result."

"Yeah... but they also say something about lighting a candle is better than cursing the dark."

Roger took his pen and jotted down a few lines on a small piece of paper he found in his briefcase. "Here is my phone number and address. Call me. We can get together and practice."

"Gracias! I'll prepare a few antiphons and psalms. Adios, Roger."

"Adios, Manuel."

Chapter 8

A van, loaded with passengers, blocked the right lane of the narrow road. Three more men were being frisked by Border Patrol agents before being loaded on the van. Two Humvees, parked on the left lane, slightly behind the van, completed the roadblock. As Roger approached the van, a man in uniform with a bullet proof vest and semi-automatic rifle stepped in front of his car. Roger rolled down the window.

"Where're you going?" asked the man. Roger looked at the passengers in the van. Six men and two women had been stopped on their way to destinations further north.

"I'm on my way to see a friend," he answered.

"Where does he live?"

"A couple of miles further south."

"What're you going to do there?"

"Practice Gregorian chants."

"You're a professional singer?" the man in uniform inquired.

"Professional? No. But I aim to improve my skills."

"Papers, please." Roger took out his driver's license.

The agent glanced at the picture and gave it back.

"OK, go slow around the vehicles. Good singing!"

The desert was wet this December morning, reveling in shiny drops dripping down the branches of mesquite and paloverde trees, in fresh pools of water in rock crevices, and diamonds of water hanging on dried yucca stalks. Baboquivari emerged from its morning shower, combing its brittle bush and creosote beard. Saturated with rainwater, saguaros swelled and shrank the openings of the holes on their columns, restricting entry by resident cactus wrens and woodpeckers. High above, below the massive granite dome, the sun was dispersing the last filaments of smoky nimbus clouds caught in oaks and sparse pines.

The road followed the contours of the bajada, descending and climbing like a roller coaster in and out of dry washes. There was a dirt road on the left that took off toward the heights of Baboquivari Peak. Roger slowed down, preparing to take it up to Manuel's hermitage. Just before the turn, he caught sight of the hood of a car parked on the right side, half hidden behind an ocotillo cactus. It had markings of the Tohono O'odham police on it. Two men in uniform sitting in it watched him with great interest as he shifted his car into four wheel drive, anticipating the steep ascent to the heights where he could now make out something like a roof.

As he climbed higher, the smell of brittlebush caressed his nostrils. After two steep but straight passages, he saw a large ramada looming above. Three switchbacks later he came out on a flat area where Manual's house sat. Manuel came out to greet him. "Bienvenido a mi casita, Roger. It's no hacienda, but it's a refuge for me."

Roger stretched his legs. "With this access road you don't need a guard dog to keep strangers away."

"It only keeps tourists away," laughed Manuel. "Amigos, they're always welcome!"

"It looks like you are well guarded, anyway. There is a police car down by your road, and a small army of Border Patrol guys a bit further. They picked up a vanload of illegals."

Manuel walked toward the ramada. From there he could see the whole valley below. The police car had left.

The ramada was still wet. Two wooden chairs were waiting for them, covered with rough horse blankets. They sat down near a small table where Manuel had set two glasses and a carafe of cranberry juice.

Huge wings glided through the mist that covered Baboquivari and circled, scanning the slope towards the south. "Buzzards are on patrol again," remarked Manuel. "They've been very active the last two days. There must be carrion not too far from here."

"What kind of buzzards are they?"

"Turkey vultures. Usually they're gone by this time of the year, although I saw caracaras the other day. Those birds are like me, they like the solitude of Baboquivari. They're still hanging around."

On the western horizon, the sun illuminated the jagged peaks of the Ajo range, making them look surrealistic. A world of hellish cataclysm in the past, now epitomizing peaceful coexistence among minerals, plants, animals, and a place of staging for migrating humans.

"I told the Border Patrol agent who stopped me earlier that I was going to meet somebody to practice Gregorian chant, and he took it in stride. He wished us good singing," said Roger.

"You never know where you can make friends," laughed Manuel, as he filled the glasses with cranberry juice. "It's that extraction of good from bad events that I want to sing about," he continued. "My nephew, Rodrigo, is here with me. The bad thing is that he was used as a mule to deliver drugs by who knows what group of traffickers. He never knew who was behind it. He carried drugs from one contact to another. Never kept the merchandise more than an hour or so. Something went wrong with the last delivery. His contact gave him a shipment, then called him to tell him the police were waiting for him at his house. Rodrigo stopped here and begged me to help him hide the load. I don't know why—maybe I took it as a sign that I should help him—I never helped him before, I took his shipment and hid it."

"You still have it?"

"Yep! Hid it in a place where nobody can find it. I didn't tell Rodrigo, either. It's too dangerous. He got a death threat right away. If he returns the stuff, they'll kill him. Here the police are watching, as you saw. By the same token, the drug dealers can't get to him. It's a stalemate. It's OK now, but it can't last. That's why I'm so eager to find a way out. You said you believe, like Kino, that even bad things happen to bring good things to those who trust in Providence's celestial favors. But in this mess, I tried to protect Rodrigo, and it's a real death trap. Was I wrong? Is there a way out?"

Roger frowned, then massaged his chin, thinking. This was a test for both of them. It was a tough situation. Now the police and Border Patrol knew he came to see Manuel. So he was involved, to a degree. When things are dark, turn toward the light. Where there is doubt, a firmer commitment to trusting Providence is called for. There was nothing obvious he could recommend, except patience and confidence.

"What we have to do, is to do nothing. We wait."

"Not too long, I hope," sighed Manuel. He realized he now sounded like Rodrigo. Patience can be the most exacting virtue. It requires reserves of faith, trust, and hope that can drain every supply of courage.

"We wait for a celestial favor," explained Roger. "This may

sound mad, but it's in our stopping our action that we will allow the celestial favor to crystallize. We don't see what it can be, but it will surely come."

"Only two of us are in this—three with Kino. That's too few. We need more singers. More voices to keep us calm and confident. We are carried, maybe like lambs. But what's our destination?"

"We trust it's a good thing. You're right, we need more singers. With them will come more indications. Patience, until then."

Manuel refilled the glasses. Roger reached for his drink. A squeak, chirp and pop froze his hand in mid motion. A male Anna hummingbird stopped a few inches from the glass of red berry juice, hesitated a few seconds, then zinged away to perch on a bare yucca stalk protruding from a patch of rosy Santa Rita prickly pear. Roger and Manuel stood to observe closer. The Anna glanced at them with one eye, then the other, flashed his iridescent pink throat to dazzle them, rose vertically to hover five feet above their heads, and darted away horizontally, disappearing in the brilliant air and warm breeze drifting from the valley below.

Granite rocks pierced the eroded mountain pediment, tumbling precipitously in places, flattening into terraces elsewhere. The buzzards in search of a meal had vacated the heights.

Footsteps on the gravel path between the house and the ramada made their heads turn toward the intruder. It was Rodrigo.

"Here's my sobrino, Rodrigo," Manuel introduced him. "Rodrigo, this is Roger."

"Hello, Rodrigo!"

"Howdy!"

"Where are you going?" asked Manuel.

"To explore the mountainside. I made me a sandwich. Have a nice day, both of you."

"Nice to meet you, Rodrigo," said Roger.

"Likewise!"

He walked off on a barely visible track made by animals, bordered on both sides by encroaching cholla cactus. He disappeared from view.

The sun was now transiting at its midday point. The air vibrated with light shimmering from a world washed clean, with bird songs from invisible throats all around— phainopeplas, cactus wrens, quails. Breezes sighed through the ramada roof. It was a song of gratitude for the beauty of creation, all participants blending perfectly in a choir.

Manuel and Roger walked to the house to have lunch.

Rodrigo followed the paths crisscrossing the mountain side. Walking on the soft ground, he was savoring the clarity of the air after the rain, the pungent smell of desert bushes, and the bracing scent of oak and pine descending from the heights.

He appreciated his uncle's help. Nevertheless, he reassured himself about the wisdom of his decision not to stay any longer. Soon it would be time to leave.

His eyes caught a motion and he froze. A white-tailed buck sprang from behind the mesquite tree where he had been napping, legs straight as pogo sticks, and effortlessly bounced behind a cover of rocks.

How long before he could resume his lucrative business with his suppliers? How to explain what happened to the previous shipment? But today he would enjoy the clear cool day, the smells and the sights.

A sweet odor intensified as he came to a clump of mesquite

trees. High in the top of the trees, blossoms of desert mistletoe filled the air with their honey fragrance. As a child he would take long sticks and knock down clusters of them to bring to his mother to enjoy. Happy days when his needs were all provided for. Does adulthood necessarily mean mistrust, fight for survival, and constant watch for signs of impending doom? He had been trained to ask no questions. The less he knew, the more efficient the business. He had no real value in the transaction—only the merchandise counted. Now the transaction was cancelled, and he felt he was to be cancelled too. Would they just gun him down on sight if he tried to contact his partners? He had to escape and run. But where?

He heard a faint whirring of birds' wings and a shadow passed over him for an instant. A vulture swooped past his head and continued gliding down toward a clump of paloverdes about a mile away. It landed, and Rodrigo saw two more there. One was walking in circles on the ground. Now the birds walked deliberately toward the tall grass thicket under the trees. He wished he had brought his uncle's binoculars. A dead deer, he thought. The vultures were very hesitant, approaching, then stopping, and retreating again. He walked over, to the great dismay of the vultures. They took off heavily and glided to the tops of two tall saguaros, where they perched. They had crests and white necks. They were caracaras.

When about fifty feet away, his stomach contracted and his pulse beat madly. Under the trees, lying face down, was a human body, apparently dead. He hesitated, but his curiosity was too strong. He came closer. It was a woman. Gray hair and part of the face he could see showed her to be about sixty. The wind picked up slightly and the smell of death reached his nose and made him run, retching to clear his lungs. He was a good four miles away from his uncle's home.

He took the small path leading directly back, going at a fast jog. A mile from his goal, he slowed down to catch his breath. Perspiring heavily, he stopped to drink one of his bottles of water. Soon he was jogging again and the ramada's top was in sight. Another quarter mile and he would be there.

He saw something red under a cat claw acacia and ignored it because he figured it was the fruit of desert Christmas cactus blooming at this time of the year. But right next to it was something yellow, and under it was something green, a sort of poncho. His heart beat fast and he had to stop. Sweat pouring into his eyes prevented him from seeing clearly until he wiped his eyes. Lying there was a man wearing green rain gear, on his back, a knapsack with a yellow water bottle in it. He was hallucinating, the mirage had to dissipate. He came closer. There was indeed a man there. To his horror the body moved, eyes looked at him fixedly, and a voice murmured, *"Ayuda me. No puedo andar."*

Rodrigo, paralyzed, stayed still.

"You speak English?" said the man. "Help me, I can't walk."

The afternoon sun was drying the last traces of rain. Songs of doves, calls of flickers and cactus wrens, raucous yells of ravens filled the air. Manuel and Roger remained silent, looking south where Mexico lay, across a geology shaped by earthquakes and now frozen in time, a place seemingly devoid of population, forgotten by history. Now it was a place where thousands of people risked their lives in a migration northward. A place where the future of two nations would be shaped by events that started long ago, not yet understood; the way a tremor that originates deep in the earth takes some time to be detected at the surface. Manuel broke the silence.

"It's deceiving how peaceful it looks down there. The shock waves made by the immigrants and drug smugglers have reached all the way up here. I've tried to ignore it. Now I'm caught in it."

"We're all in it. The whole nation has tried to ignore it. Neglecting what's going on down there is going to cause a lot of trouble."

Suddenly Rodrigo's voice interrupted their conversation. "Tio, come see! Somebody needs help!"

"What's the matter, Rodrigo?" asked Manuel. "Who needs help?"

"He's just below our road! He says he can't walk. He looks sick or something. And there's a dead woman way down there a few miles away."

"What are you talking about?" Manuel almost shouted.

"Let's go and help the guy first," responded Rodrigo. "He is alive. We have to take care of him."

They hurried behind Rodrigo and in a few minutes they were looking at a form in a green rain poncho, under the cat claw acacia. The form turned and they saw a man in his mid-forties, brown skin, heavy mustache, jet black hair, an expression of intense pain on his face. He attempted to stand but gave up, groaning in disgust.

"I can't move. Can you get me someplace where somebody take a look at my knee?"

"Should we call an ambulance?" Roger asked.

The man's eyes filled with fear. "No! Por favor, don't! Can you help me quietly? No ambulance, no police, please."

"Where are you from?" asked Manuel.

"I'm not an illegal. I'm from Mexico. My name is Miguel—Miguel Aguilar. Take me to a shelter and let me rest a while. I can pay, I have dollars."

Manuel looked at Rodrigo and Roger. "OK, we will take you to my house and we will talk."

All three lifted the man carefully. He could not put any weight on his right leg.

"Ay! I screwed up my knee! I hope it's not broken."

Manuel and Rodrigo joined their hands, crossed their forearms and made Miguel sit in that makeshift chair while Roger grabbed him around the chest and held him up straight. They carried him slowly toward the house.

"Lucky we don't have to go far. Another quarter mile and you'd have made it to our house," said Rodrigo.

"Two days I've been here. Last night I thought it was going to be my last. I kept passing out and I was shivering. I yelled, but nobody heard me. I saw a car drive up this morning and yelled again. Nobody stopped."

They made it to the house, put him on the enormous aspen bed and removed his boots. They tried rolling up his jeans to his knee, but the knee was too swollen and Miguel cried out in pain. Rodrigo undid the belt buckle and all three lifted his waist up and pulled the jeans down to the knees. The knee was swollen twice its size, blue with brown tinges, but did not show breakage. Manuel brought a glass of water that Miguel downed in one continuous series of gulps. "More please," he murmured.

They gave him two more glasses and he began to recover. There were two enchiladas left from lunch. Manuel reheated them, and Miguel downed them in no time.

"Looks like our rescued bird will live," commented Roger.

Miguel, for the first time, smiled. They left him on the bed, and as soon as he lay down, he fell asleep.

They now turned to the other problem, the dead woman Rodrigo had reported. They piled into Manuel's truck and drove halfway there, then had to cut across the paths that Rodrigo had taken. The caracaras marked the place, and left reluctantly as the men approached. This time Rodrigo stayed behind and the other two approached the body. After verifying the body was as Rodrigo had said—that of a woman—they retreated to a distance.

"She probably was an illegal immigrant who didn't make it," reflected Roger.

"That's more and more common. This land's becoming a morgue," replied Manuel.

"What should we do with her?" asked Rodrigo.

"She doesn't need human help anymore, only prayers," answered Manuel. "If we go to La Migra, and they come out to investigate right away, they'll find Miguel. He didn't seem happy at the thought of an interview with them. First thing to do is find out more about Miguel. We'll decide what to do with her after that."

Miguel was still sleeping. Manuel quietly reached for the knapsack beside the bed and closed the door behind him. They gathered around the kitchen table. Inside the pack they found jeans, a shirt, socks, underwear, and an envelope with a handwritten note in Spanish. "May God and the Virgin of Guadalupe and of all the Americas protect you, my dear husband. Make sure you are back for Christmas in your own land, back from the cold north. The children and I will pray for you every day. With all our love. Your wife who loves you." The signature was not readable.

"He seems like a regular guy," remarked Manuel.

Carefully folded in a side pocket were topographic maps of the region, covering the land from the Mexican border to Kitt Peak and extending east to Robles Junction. Several points were circled.

"Look at this!" Rodrigo exclaimed admiringly as he found a GPS receiver in the bag. "Latest model. I wish I could afford one like that."

In a hidden pocket in the back seam was a plastic bag containing a driver's license, eight hundred and seventy-five dollars, a credit card from a U.S. bank, and documents with names and phone numbers. The U.S. driver's license showed a Glenwood Springs address in the state of Colorado, under his name—Miguel Aguilar. The credit card also had the same name on it.

"Who's this guy? What's your take on it, Roger?" wondered Manuel.

"He could be a resident of Colorado," Roger ventured. "Except for his wife's note saying he's from Mexico. That's what it implies to me at least."

"Same to me," Rodrigo added.

"So what's the best thing to do?" continued Manuel.

"We could turn him over to the police," Roger thought out loud. "He didn't seem to like the idea of calling an ambulance. He would like the police even less."

"Don't call the police," interjected Rodrigo.

"I think we need to find out who he is," interrupted Roger, "and decide where we want to go from there. Let's not make a hasty decision. I have a feeling we found another voice for your choir."

"This vagabundo? Are you kidding?"

"You never know, Manuel."

"What choir? What are you yakking about?" interrupted Rodrigo, somewhat annoyed.

"You're invited to join, too," answered Manuel. "It's a choir where we sing to give thanks for celestial favors."

"What favors?"

"Everything has a purpose," explained Roger. "As Kino would say, everything is a celestial favor."

"Now there's two of you talking about this favor nonsense!"

Obviously, Rodrigo was not volunteering to join the choir, so they talked about what to do with their uninvited guest. They agreed to let Miguel continue to sleep undisturbed. He would have to explain how he got there, later.

It was time for Roger to leave. "Call me when you find out more about him. He may be the celestial favor we need to find a way out of this maze."

Manuel shook hands with Roger. "Let's hope, then, that he turns out to be a great big favor. Vaya con Dios, amigo."

Chapter 9

The sun grazed the horizon. Rodrigo and Manuel finished dinner in silence, trying to absorb the events of the day. The big aspen bed creaked under the shifting weight of Miguel.

"Vamos! Let's go see him!" exclaimed Manuel.

Miguel had rolled, and his legs dangled from the side of the bed. He held his right knee, grimacing, feeling for the extent of the damage.

"Did you sleep?" asked Manuel.

"For a while, but the pain woke me up. I'm afraid it's not so good with my knee."

"Rodrigo, go get a couple of pain pills—above the kitchen sink, on the left side."

"Thanks for letting me rest," said Miguel.

"Take all the rest you need. You're safe here."

Rodrigo brought the pills and a glass of water.

"What are you going to do with me?" inquired Miguel.

"First, we fix you up so you feel better. Then, it depends. Tell us more about how you got here all banged up."

"I was carrying a lady on my back and tripped. I dropped her and twisted my knee. Not a smart thing to do when you plan on walking sixty kilometers without being seen."

"Wait a minute," Manuel jumped in. "Do you mean the woman who died a few miles from here?"

"Ah! You found her? She was sick. I tried to carry her some place where she would be found, but instead I became lame and she died in my arms. This trip is not going the way I had planned."

"Where were you headed?"

"Toward Robles Junction, and from there to Glenwood Springs, in Colorado."

"How were you going to get to Colorado?" interjected Rodrigo.

"I had a ride for the rest of the way."

"What are you? A coyote? You have the latest GPS gear," Rodrigo kept questioning.

"No! I have nothing to do with immigrants. I had business to do in Glenwood Springs for the Mexican government. I was to go there, stay three days, come back, and walk back the same way I came. Less than a week for the whole trip. I've got to get back to my wife and kids as soon as I can walk."

"Wait a minute! I don't get the picture," said Manuel. "Can you take it from the beginning? Help me understand."

"OK, but give me something to drink."

"How about coffee?"

"Sounds good! What do you want to know?"

"Why do you sneak in instead of coming legally, through customs?"

"I had my orders because of the business I had to do in Colorado. I was going there to negotiate how many workers were needed at gas drilling sites in Colorado. There's a big problem with our workers coming back due to the bad economy in your country. Many enlist in groups of armed drug traffickers. Governments on both sides are trying to slow down their return. We have too many unemployed workers, and the government does not pay unemployment money. Jobs now are in drug trafficking."

"Why not fly to Colorado and discuss things openly?" asked Manuel.

"It wouldn't work. The drilling companies want to increase drilling. They also want cheap and experienced workers. We have a lot of them. They are all union workers. They return and are hired by the drug cartels. Your government wants to let the energy companies rehire some of them, but both sides refuse to recognize the existence of illegal immigrants. This would ease the problem in Sonora, with fewer recruits for drug cartels, and it would help Colorado too. But nobody wants to recognize the deal officially. So they chose me to work the deal quietly. I have a legal Colorado driver's license. It's genuine. You can check."

"Why don't they give papers to the workers too?" asked Manuel.

"As illegals, they're cheaper. The workers prefer that, too. They want dollars, not immigration rights. Their families are in Mexico. In Colorado they would be paid in dollars and they can send a lot back home. They want to go home and open stores or restaurants."

"What if they're caught?"

"Small chance for that! Few are caught, and if they are, they come back. Most can turn around in a few days and start walking again. They have their own guides, provided by the organization that is sending them. They have trails mapped out and cars waiting."

"So you too work for the 'organization'?"

"No! I work for the National Geological Survey in Hermosillo. They chose me because I used to work for the oil company before, and I know the geology and maps of this terrain on both sides of the frontier, and also I can talk business with the hiring companies. I was the best candidate. Nobody sees, nobody knows. Business as usual. Politics are left to the officials on both sides."

"How many deals are made like that, in secret, by the two governments?" asked Manuel.

"It's quite common. But the question that never comes up is why do governments not deal with the real problem? Why are the people running away in the first place?"

"And if the police find you, what happens?" asked Rodrigo.

"They must not! Not only I'm in trouble but so is my whole family. Failure is not an option with jobs like mine. I can go home and come back later, but if I'm caught and the plan exposed, that is bad."

"How did you get a driver's license from Colorado?" inquired Manuel.

"I never asked how. But it's a valid one, issued by the state of Colorado."

"And your credit card?"

"Same thing. It's real."

"And that woman, the lady you carried on your back? How did you meet her?" Rodrigo asked.

"That's how things went sour. I was walking at the foot of the bajada, making excellent time. Five hours I walked, then I stopped for a quick lunch. I heard a woman's voice singing. It was strange. I knew nobody lived there. The song was about La Guadalupe. I knew immediately she was an immigrant. I thought she must be crazy to signal her position like that, and I quickly got up and started to walk away. I heard a few more words. She chanted, saying, 'Have pity on me'. She was not my problem. I could not do anything for her. But somehow I stopped, and I went back in the direction of the voice. I spied her from a distance. She was sitting on the ground, in the middle of a clump of bushes, acting like a little girl playing in her backyard. I waited to make sure she was alone and walked up to her. At first she thought I was her son, Ignacio, she called me. I told her I was just passing through. She begged me to take her to Ignacio, her son in Nebraska, in a town called La Vista, I believe. She was needed because her son's wife was expecting a baby, so they sent money for her trip. I asked her what her name was. She said Lupe Flores."

Miguel paused, sipping some coffee, then he continued. "She told me her son had emigrated to Nebraska five years ago, illegally, of course, like everybody else. He got a good job in a meat packing plant. He met a girl from Guadalajara, they got married, and now she was expecting a baby. So Lupe's son sent her money for the passage arranged by coyotes he trusted, he said. They would take her through Arizona, through Colorado, all the way to La Vista. She paid them in advance and started walking from the border. Seven men and two coyotes were with her."

Miguel looked at his listeners; their eyes were riveted on him. So he decided to give them the whole story as he had gathered it from Lupe.

"After crossing the border, Lupe and her group stopped in a place where another coyote was waiting. He told them they would have to carry an extra pack from this point on. It was instead of more money, he said. The price they paid was not correct. It now cost more, all the way to Nebraska. So they could either pay five thousand dollars more, or carry this little pack for a few hours, not more than four hours maximum. That was a good bargain since nobody had any money left.

"Lupe and her group started to walk. After about five kilometers, the extra pack became heavy. She asked one of the men with her what it was and he said it was probably drugs. Another two kilometers and she decided to leave one of her water containers behind after drinking as much as she could from it. Then she got sore ankles. She was always bothered by sore ankles, she told me, if she walked too fast. She asked one of the coyotes if they could stop for a minute. 'Sure, lady. Let's stop,' he said.

"She sat down and took her shoes off and rubbed her ankles. The lead coyote turned and snapped at her, 'Lady, this is not a massage parlor. You walk with us or you walk on your own.' That scared her, so she quickly got back on her feet and rejoined the march. But an hour later she could not stand the pain again. She asked for another rest stop. This time the coyotes talked to each other and they stopped. 'OK,' they said, 'everybody, take five minutes. No more.'

"They came to her and gave her two pills they told her would relieve the pain. Lupe said she took them and immediately felt better. But soon after, she felt very sleepy. The lead coyote came to her and said words she could not hear. He waved his hand in front of her eyes and disappeared. She noticed that the group got up and started to walk again. When she woke up she was all alone and felt dizzy. She could barely stand up; everything was turning slowly.

"They had taken her bottles of water. The night was falling. She started to cry. She pulled herself up and walked toward the mountains she saw, and walked as long as she could, in the dimming light. Suddenly she saw a tinaja, knelt down and drank some of the water. It tasted brackish but was refreshing to her burning mouth. She passed out again. When she woke up, her insides were burning with fever, her abdomen hurt everywhere. Unable to move, she spent a day or two there, half-conscious. Then she felt very weak, and knew she was dying. She started to sing the song to La Guadalupe: 'Now and at the hour of our death.'

"That's when I heard her," declared Miguel. "I figured I

could carry her and drop her off near the road, which was only a couple of kilometers away. There either La Migra or some local residents might find her eventually. So I picked her up on my back and we started toward the road. She was praying for me and her son. I carried her for a while. Suddenly, my foot slipped, and I tried to regain my balance by shifting her weight abruptly. My right knee got completely twisted and we both fell heavily. She fell on me. I had to extricate my knee from underneath her. I got up. I was in pain, and I could not continue toward the road. I decided to stay where we were and rest my knee. As I rested, the knee became stiffer and stiffer. We were in trouble. I shared my evening meal with her and we talked. She asked me to write to her son and gave me his address, written on an envelope she had hidden in her overcoat. 'Miguel, I won't see my son and grandchild, I'm going to die here,' she said.

"I told her to hang on. We would figure out something next morning. I sat next to her, and she rested her head in my lap. We talked into the night. She was beginning to hallucinate. Then she was lucid again. After midnight, she became silent. Before long, I fell asleep. When I woke up, rain was falling. I looked at Lupe and saw she was dead. I had nothing to bury her with, so I left and crawled for hours. My progress was very slow. All day I crawled and barely went six kilometers. That night, I ate my last food bar and started to pray like Lupe. Next day, the rain stopped, but I couldn't move anymore. That's when you found me under the tree."

All three remained silent for a while.

"So you help her and this is what happens to you?" Rodrigo commented sarcastically.

"What would you have done, amigo? When a fellow human being is in need, do you just walk away?" responded Miguel.

"How do you know what she was carrying was drugs?"

pursued Rodrigo.

"She said so. More and more, it is becoming the rule with coyotes. Even if not in a drug cartel, coyotes want a part of the action. They prefer drugs to people. They use immigrants as burros to carry their stuff. A disabled burro becomes a danger for them, and they abandon it without hesitation."

"That's the ugly side of drugs," cut in Rodrigo. "I think of it as a game played by bored people from large cities, and if they want to play, well, let them play. The drug business is supply and demand. Some demand, others supply. It's capitalism."

Miguel and Manuel waited in silence for more from Rodrigo. But he fell silent, as if carrying some unspoken guilt.

"What do you want us to do with you?" asked Manuel.

"I can't continue. I have to go back as soon as I can. My ride did not wait for me. The driver was supposed to meet me two days ago. The only thing to do is slip back the same way I came and replan the trip. But I need time to get my knee working again."

"How is it this morning?"

"Better than yesterday, for sure, but not good enough to walk yet. I need more time."

Rodrigo felt somewhat edgy. "How about the dead lady, Lupe?" he asked.

"We have to bury her," responded Miguel.

"That's not going to work," said Manuel. "You'll leave, but she'll stay here. If bones are discovered, that's not unusual around here. That's an everyday matter, and nobody questions, but if a grave is discovered, we who live here have a lot of questions to answer. So first, we must decide if we leave her body as it is, or if we call the police. They'll take care of the body. What do you think, Miguel?"

"We can't leave her like that. We have to bury her."

"No, Miguel. If your choice is not to let her stay there, that's good, but it means we call the police."

"They'll find me, and I'm in big trouble. My wife and kids and whole family are in big trouble!"

"Relax, Miguel. The police won't find you. I guarantee you that. I have a place for you where nobody will find you if you stay hidden until I come to get you."

"So! I'll finally know where you have hidden my lousy merchandise!" exclaimed Rodrigo.

Miguel looked puzzled, his eyes questioning.

"You'll understand later, Miguel," Manuel said. "Right now we have to plan your disappearance and how we handle the police."

Manuel went into the tool shed behind the house and came back a half-hour later with improvised wooden crutches. "Try these and tell me if you can hobble comfortably using them."

Miguel took the crutches and moved around the room, slowly at first. In a few minutes he was hopping around with assurance.

"Great!" said Manuel. "We don't have to carry you. Just be careful. Where we're going is pretty dark. Here," he gave him a flashlight, "you will need this. Put it in your pocket."

"Where we going?" asked Rodrigo.

"Patience, young man! Help me make a sandwich and fill two bottles of water. Miguel has to be comfortable in his hiding place. Take the other flashlight so our guest can see the way."

They walked out in the dusky evening and started to climb slowly above the house, Miguel maneuvering his bum knee carefully around loose stones and rocks that covered the ground. After five hundred yards, they stopped in front of a boulder four feet high. Behind it was a flat rock half hidden by another rounded boulder, this one of imposing size, large as a house. Behind this large boulder, the slope rose almost vertically for two hundred feet. From where they stood, they could see the whole valley and the Tohono O'odham lands as far as the Quijotoa Mountains. They walked on the flat rock and came to the large boulder.

"Here we are," said Manuel.

"Where we going?" asked Rodrigo again.

"Look in front of you," replied Manuel.

"I don't see anything."

"Look behind the brittlebush growing down there, against the rock. "

"It's too dark," complained Rodrigo.

"Follow me," said Manuel.

They stepped from the flat rock down in the darkness of the large boulder. Behind the brittlebush, there was an opening about the size of a man crouching, leading under the boulder. Manuel took the flashlight from Miguel and shone the beam into the opening.

"Do you feel the air moving? It's from a cave. It's much bigger inside. Follow me. It gets bigger after a while so you can stand up."

Manuel entered the mouth of the cave. Miguel sat down and, using his arms and one leg, backed carefully into the opening. Rodrigo followed him with the crutches. After crawling about thirty feet, Manuel illuminated a little grotto where, keeping shoulders hunched and heads low, they could almost stand up. Manuel then took a narrow passageway about fifty feet long that opened up into a cave about a hundred feet high and half an acre in area. He waited for Rodrigo to get in and painted the walls with the beam of the flashlight. In the silence, a drip could be heard. Manuel shone the spotlight on a stalactite hanging from the ceiling of the cave.

"Be careful! Don't go to the right. Stay to the left," ordered Manuel.

On the left side, stalactites of various sizes could be seen, slowly dripping. The drops fell for a few seconds and hit a water surface far below, making a faint plopping sound. Rodrigo whistled softly. "Boy! It must be deep down there."

"I measured about a hundred and fifty feet one day," explained Manuel. "You don't want to fall in it; this water is feeding our well. But it's deeper on the other side." He shone the light on the ground. Between them and the edge, where the waterfall dropped into the pool feeding the well, man-size rocks had fallen from the ceiling and formed a protective barrier about a foot tall in most places. "Don't go too close, you never know."

Then he shone the light straight ahead. A platform about twenty feet wide, covered with travertine, extended to the other side of the cave. It showed traces of a mineral spring that had dried up.

"Look at this." The beam of the flashlight ran along the floor and disappeared, swallowed by darkness. "Get closer, but stay behind me!"

The whole floor of the cave had collapsed and a chasm opened up, with no bottom visible. Manuel picked up a piece of loose travertine and threw it into the abyss. They counted the seconds—one... two... three... four. Then the stone hit something and ricocheted faintly and all was quiet.

"Wow! That is deep!" exclaimed Rodrigo.

"Now look at this," continued Manuel. The beam of his flashlight crawled along the floor to a small round alcove about fifteen feet in diameter and ten feet high. Piled neatly in the back were plastic bags.

"That's where they are!" blurted out Rodrigo.

"I hope they stay here forever," said Manuel.

"What's in the bags?" asked Miguel.

"Rodrigo's sins—pot!" exclaimed Manuel.

Manuel walked up to the pile of plastic bags, took out several from the middle, and placed them on both ends to make a sort of small sofa.

"Here, Miguel, here's your throne. Sit on it and make yourself comfortable. I hope you're not afraid of the dark. There's nothing in here except bats and ringtail cats. You can see their droppings along the wall."

"Have you seen them?" asked Miguel.

"That's how I discovered the cave. When I first came here to choose a place to build my house, one evening at sunset, I was sitting near the boulders outside. I saw some animal move like lightning and disappear. It had a long nose and a large fluffy tail. A miner's cat. I walked to see where it went and found no trace of it. I came back during daylight and searched the base of the boulder and discovered the entrance to his cave. I saw that the water level in here was about fifty feet below the place I was planning to build my house. That gave me hope to hit water if I drilled a well. I was right. The drill hit water sixty feet deep, right where I estimated the pool of water to be located. That ringtail cat showed me the secret to finding water all the way up here."

"How long you want me to sit here in the dark?" asked Miguel.

"You can come out. Just stay behind the boulders. Rodrigo is going to talk to the police, since he found Lupe. But when you see police cars way down in the valley, you crawl back in here and stay out of sight. Don't come out until I come to get you myself."

"OK, Jefe," promised Miguel.

The next morning, the tribal police and La Migra followed Rodrigo to the place where Lupe's body was resting. A van arrived shortly after, and they took pictures and carried away the body. Then Rodrigo and Manuel had to give a deposition, fill out official papers, and sign them. By mid-afternoon it was all done. The police drove off.

Manuel and Rodrigo waited until close to sunset. They climbed back to the cave and found Miguel sitting on the pile of plastic bags.

"They're gone. Lupe's body's gone. You're safe, Miguel," announced Manuel.

"That's good news. Thank you. I owe you a lot. But I have not so good news. These bags do not contain pot only—some of this stuff is cocaine, amigos. You're in bigger trouble than you thought."

"What? What are you talking about? How do you know that?" Rodrigo cried out.

Miguel got up, steadied himself on his crutches, fished out the flashlight from his pocket and shone it on two bags he had set aside on top of the pile.

"See this scribbling on the bags?"

"Looks like a V and a C with a circle around. What does that mean?" asked Rodrigo.

"Every third bag or so has this marking. After you left, I started moving bags around, and it did not take long to find the first one with this logo. It means Vera Cruz. It's an organization that controls shipping and distribution of cocaine from South America. The product comes into the port of Vera Cruz. From there, it's trucked in government trucks to places near the border."

"What? The Mexican government is into drugs?" blurted out

Rodrigo.

"No. But the drug cartels are very powerful. They have infiltrators in the army, and they use army trucks to move their stuff. From the border, it is carried across mostly by other cartel members using people who returned and could not find any jobs. To a small extent, they use illegal immigrants like my poor Lupe. When I worked for the oil company at Chicontepec, I had direct contact with officials of the oil workers' union. I became aware of the other product some of them handled. It wasn't oil, it was cocaine. That's when I first saw this logo. They wanted to recruit me. My wife and I decided we wanted no part of it. I asked for an assignment to Hermosillo, far away from Vera Cruz, where there was an opening for a geologist at the University of Sonora. When I was asked to volunteer for this trip, the people who gave me my driver's license and credit card were from Vera Cruz. That's why I want to return to Hermosillo without a hitch. I want no trouble with these people."

"Cocaine! My suppliers lied to me!" Rodrigo was dejected. "That's why the load was twice as much as usual."

"That changes everything," said Manuel. "Rodrigo, we have to get rid of this merchandise, quick!"

"Can't we just return it?" Rodrigo pleaded.

"Who gave this to you?" asked Miguel.

"A guy named Sureño. I don't know much about him. He's new around here."

"That's a phony name," affirmed Miguel. "That's how they operate. You don't know who your contact really is, only his voice and his face. Everyone is nameless, receives orders and executes them like a robot. You cannot return anything, Rodrigo. If you try, you will be eliminated. Who paid you?"

"Del Norte. I don't know him either."

"Another phony name! You cannot quit this organization. If

you don't deliver the goods, you're dead."

Rodrigo's world was dissolving, his hopes dripping like drops of blood from the stalactites into a bottomless abyss. His decision not to deliver the merchandise severed not just his relationship with nameless employers, it severed his neck. He saw himself dead as that Lupe woman, surrounded by vultures. He was in the company of countless men and women whose decapitated bodies were found all over the bajada in dry arroyos, under mesquite trees or in shallow graves. He had become one of them.

"Rodrigo, trust me, you're not alone. I'm with you. You can count on me." Manuel had to shake his arm to get him out of his paralyzing fear.

"What are we going to do?" Rodrigo blurted out.

"Simple. I almost did it when I carried this pile of junk in here," answered Manuel. "We throw it in the deep well on the right. I did not want to do it without your OK. But let's do it now. Agreed?"

"I want nothing to do with this stuff. Let's get rid of it."

Rodrigo carried the bags and stashed them near the edge of the precipice. Manuel heaved them into the abyss. With each bag that disintegrated on the sides of the chasm, Rodrigo felt freer. Miguel sat on the ground and watched. A few minutes of hard work, and the whole shipment of drugs splattered against the rocks at the bottom of the well.

"I hope your ringtail doesn't find the cocaine," said Miguel. "I think I heard it rummaging nearby in the dark. Every time I turned on the light it remained silent."

"They're smarter than people about things like that. He'll be fine," Manuel reassured him.

The job done, they emerged from the cave after sunset and went back to the house.

By the time Manuel finished cooking tamales, it was completely dark. After dinner, Miguel sat down to keep his promise to Lupe to write to her son, Ignacio, in faraway Nebraska.

My dear son Ignacio,

By the time you get this letter, I will be long gone. I have asked this gentleman to write you a few lines to tell you how I died. The most important is that I died without fear and with love for you, your wife, and the niño to be born soon. I died without regret. I wanted to come help you but God wanted it otherwise. Let His will be done. I died with the help of La Guadalupe. She will help me when I get to the other side and will intercede for me with her son. I do not hate the coyotes that poisoned me. They could have explained to me that it was necessary to do what they did. I was unable to walk. You know how I have this problem with my ankles. I was too slow and the others could not be put in danger because of me. I had to be sacrificed so others could go on. I accept this. Let me be sacrificed so that you, my darling son, can live better. Live in the love of the Son of God.

I drank bad water in this desert and became very sick. Now I am so thirsty! I thirst for you and your niño. I also thirst for the other niño who will be born at Christmas, very soon, our Jesus, whom I will meet even sooner.

I am a dust devil twisting and disappearing in the desert. I am a sign nobody seems to read. I come, I burn,

I die, and no one understands. I am a warning nobody wants to hear, a sight nobody wants to see. I am like a lamb led to the slaughter yards of the north.

My Ignacio, remember who you are. You have in you the blood of your ancestors who were all people who believed in God and prayed to La Guadalupe, the patroness of all the Americas. She chose us—our country. She wanted us to pray for all its inhabitants, to always be faithful to her son. Remember your family who fought and died for their faith, so that Cristo Rey would always be honored in our land. Remember my father's uncle who was a priest and was shot by those who wanted to make our country a country without hope and without love. You come from a family with strong faith. Nobody can defeat us. One thing I ask of you in this foreign country: do not forget who you are, do not become changed by your new surroundings. You are a subject of Cristo Rey. Always love La Guadalupe. You will not have me as mother anymore. She will be your mother now.

Strange, when death comes, it is not frightening. It is like an opening to something bigger. It is here. It is an immense hope. I see it as a new beginning, something that requires a great sacrifice. It brings me a joy I never felt before. I am sure La Guadalupe is here with me. My head is resting on her knees. She, who held her dead son like this, is now holding me the same way.

I have a little something here I have knitted myself for the niño. I am sure it is a boy but just in case it is a girl, I knitted it in yellow, like for a baby chick.

La Guadalupe, who is holding me, promised she will send it to you. I die happy, my son, my Ignacio.

P.S. Dear Sir,

I found your mother in the desert and tried to carry her to a shelter but I twisted my knee and could not carry her any further. She died with her head on my lap. She talked to me as if I were her son at first, and toward the end as if I were La Guadalupe. I hope you forgive me. I tried to write it like she said it to me, but I am not nearly as tender and loving, and I am sure I betrayed the greatness of her joy because of the dullness of my mind. I did not understand some other things she told me. You have a great mother. She gave me your address. I hope this letter reaches you and finds you in good health.

Miguel Aguilar.

Miguel folded the letter and addressed it. "Manuel, can you mail this for me?"

"Sure, Miguel."

"And here is a little something Lupe knitted for her grandchild. Could you wrap it and send it also?" Then he took out a twenty dollar bill and gave it to Manuel. "Here, this should cover the expenses, I believe. Please take it."

Chapter 10

"Quiburi is burning!" yelled the two scouts as they galloped back to Chief Coro's waiting group of warriors. Coro led the way to the summit of the hill. Ten miles away, the Pima village of Quiburi, on the banks of the San Pedro River, was veiled in billowing black smoke. Flames could be seen in places consuming what was left of the houses.

"Apaches!" shouted Coro in disgust. "We've got to punish them!"

Coro's troop of sixty men stared in angry silence at the charred remains of their village. Nothing had worked out well during this expedition. Their northern cousins had refused to send reinforcements of warriors to organize a counter attack against the enemy. Moving deeply into Pima territory, Apaches and Janos, their allies, multiplied lightning raids against Pima settlements, stealing horses and killing men, women, and children. Despite a promise of support from their famous friend, the missionary Kino, who was rounding up Spanish soldiers to come to their aid, the northern tribes had refused to join them, arguing that they could not afford to leave their own villages unprotected. Lack of unity among the Pimas emboldened their enemies. They came in ever larger numbers, sacking isolated settlements. And now it had been Quiburi's turn, the home of Chief Coro. Coro had risked taking half his men with him to the North, leaving the others to defend the village. His mistake was gnawing at his belly.

The warriors approached the smoldering village cautiously, circling it and then rushing from all sides. No trace of Apaches. The attack had come from the east, according to the trackers. They found two scalped men's corpses there. In the village center, three elderly women lay dead, their heads cracked open. Everybody else had disappeared. There were numerous tracks, among them those of women and children, leading southwest toward Huachuca, and other tracks, apparently of Apache warriors, leading north.

After burying the dead, the men put out the fires still burning and set up camp on a bluff, by the river, on a place easily defended. Coro set up watches for the night, four men at a time, to guard against any surprise. The moon set and it became pitch dark.

Coro awakened from a shallow sleep. He heard footsteps. He grabbed his bow and arrows, and made sure his stout heavy club was at his side. A dozen men were approaching stealthily from the south. Coro was ready to shout an alarm when he recognized one of his own men leading them, signaling his coming with both hands raised. The camp awakened in an instant and gathered around the newcomers. They were part of the warriors Coro had left behind to guard the village. Cegia, the shaman, was the leader. They related how the raid had occurred. As instructed by Coro, they had set up a ring of watchmen around the village. The Apaches came brazenly, walking openly, in full daylight, shortly after noon, as if they knew that the place was not fully manned by warriors. They came in strength, about a hundred men. The watchmen detected their coming about two miles from the village. When the men learned of their superior numbers, they ordered the people to flee immediately toward Chief Taravala's fortified town at Huachuca. Women, children, and the elderly took what they could of their possessions and ran, with the warriors covering the retreat. Cegia stayed behind with ten men and returned at night to scout on the enemy, only to find Coro's watchmen.

"How many men did we lose?" questioned Coro.

"Two are missing. They were working in the fields and decided to run back to get some of their belongings. We warned them to come with us, but they ran back. We haven't seen them yet."

"They're dead," announced Coro. "And the old women?" Cegia's warriors did not know about them.

"What news about our brothers from the North?" inquired Cegia.

"They refused to join us. They believe they can survive on their own. Big mistake. There's no unity among the Pimas. We're at the mercy of the Apaches until we strike back. We have to strike now!"

"We can strike," reflected Cegia, "when we unite with our people at Huachuca, and wait for the arrival of the Spanish Cavalry that Kino is bringing. Then we can wipe them out."

"We'll not find them, then. They'll be in their mountains, hidden in the rocks. The Cavalry will return to their garrisons and our people to Huachuca. Then we'll be attacked again and again, until we flee or are wiped out. We must strike now, on our own land."

"Seventy of us against at least a hundred? We survived with little loss, but if we attack now they'll finish us. Quiburi will be no more."

"We mustn't lose. We'll win."

"Are you the Spirit? You see in the future?"

"No, but I can tell you why we keep losing. We're not a

people, we don't have a common soul, and we pull in different directions. We're afraid to die. We wait for the Spaniards to act for us. We're afraid to meet head to head with our death, whatever name it has—Apaches, Jocomes... and now the Apaches attacked us. They defied us to respond. We must respond if we want to infuse a soul in our people. The enemy is watching us, and so are our people, to see if we can stand up again as one."

"What do you propose we do?" hesitated Cegia.

"Track them down. Teach them who we are."

A shiver went through the warriors. Some jumped up ready to follow Coro, others loudly stated it was wiser to wait. Cegia asked to be heard again.

"We don't have that common soul Chief Coro talked about. If we attack, divided as we are, we'll lose, since they far outnumber us. I say we track them and find out where they're going. We need more men to fight them, so let's send two of us to call the rest of our warriors from Huachuca, and at least a dozen more volunteers. When they're here, then, together we attack the enemy."

A heated discussion followed, but eventually they agreed it was a worthy scheme. Reluctantly, Coro also agreed.

Coro's disunited group left Quiburi, following their trackers. Soon the trail of footprints left by the enemy was picked up, following the San Pedro on the east side, headed northward. By midday they could tell that the Apache raiders were only about an hour ahead of them. Cegia became alarmed. That was not what he expected. He had counted on a slow pursuit, giving time for reinforcement to arrive from Huachuca, in two or three days. But the Apaches had other ideas. They were going at a very leisurely pace, as on a hunting trip, stopping here and there and circling back before moving on. By mid-afternoon, the trackers found some clear footprints still full of water in the sand near a marshy area. They estimated they were no more than half an hour old. Coro and Cegia decided to have the troop take a rest to leave some distance between them and the raiders. They sat down in a dry clearing next to the marsh.

Suddenly the trackers, hidden in bushes at the edge of the marsh, crawled back, alarmed. Using hand signals, they informed the group that some Apaches were coming their way. Everybody lay low while Coro and Cegia crawled forward to study the oncoming danger.

Coro peered through the dense vegetation and saw two warriors, one looking like a chief. Cegia whispered in Coro's ear, "It's Achak, the leader of the Apaches that devastate our lands." Coro watched Achak as he came up from the marsh and set foot on a small dry island. Unable to watch any longer, he jumped up and yelled at the enemy.

"Achak, I am Coro, chief of the Pimas. You burned our village. It's time for you to pay. I challenge you to fight me. Accept, if you're not a worthless coyote."

Achak, surprised, first started to run, then stopped to look at his challenger standing on the other side of the marsh. "You want to die, Pima?"

"I'm not afraid to die, Achak. I came to make you pay for your crimes."

The enemy groups were gathered on the perimeter of the marsh, with Achak on the island in the center. You could tell they were quite a few on both sides, without being able to count them accurately because of the bushes and dense vegetation.

"How do you want to die, Pima? Choose your weapon."

Coro lifted his stout, heavy club. "This is fitting to kill a coyote like you, Achak."

Achak asked for a similar club to be brought to him. His companions swiftly supplied him with one. Coro waded through the marsh to the island, holding his club high.

He circled around Achak carefully, club in hand. With a savage shout, Achak ran straight at him. Coro adroitly stepped aside and kicked Achak's leg, sending him to the ground. But Achak rolled like a cat, and in a smooth motion got back on his feet. Coro resumed his circling. Suddenly, he jumped at his enemy. Achak bent down low, grabbed Coro at the waist, lifted him up, and sent him tumbling behind his back. Before he could turn around to face him, Coro was on his feet, club held high. Coro circled again, observing Achak. Every time Coro stepped forward, Achak crouched down, attempting to club his enemy's knees or belly. The gladiators were taking measure of each other, preparing for a fatal blow.

Cegia was beside himself with rage. If Coro got killed, the Apaches would attack them, and with their numeric advantage, the Pimas would find themselves in an uneven fight. Even if Coro won, attacking with such inferior strength would be suicide. He watched Coro, riveted to every move.

Coro kept lunging forward, forcing Achak to bend down to avoid his powerful blows. All Pima eyes were on their chief who did not hesitate to put his life on the line. Each man thought: He is doing it for Quibury, for all the losses and humiliations at the hand of Achak. He is sacrificing himself for me, for our families, for those who ran to Huachuca, for those who refused to join them, up there to the north, for the soul of the whole nation. If he can die, we can too. If he wins, we will win. Each lunge and retreat against Achak is a movement toward a common destiny, a movement away from self-interest. Coro is the chief, yet his life is the only one now on the line, given for all of them without holding back.

Coro made another patented move and Achak responded

with his usual tactic, bending the knee, aiming low at Coro. Except this time, Coro danced to the right, jumped high, and landed at the side of Achak, and with one incredible blow, split his enemy's forehead open. Achak fell to his knees and bent awkwardly back, staring grotesquely at the sky, motionless.

Suddenly Cegia jumped up shrieking, "Pimas, for our land, for our loved ones, for our victorious Chief Coro—no mercy!"

The marsh exploded with Pimas materializing from the midst of bushes, yelling, bows firing arrows, lances piercing Apache backs and clubs breaking bones. It was over in a few minutes. The San Pedro flowed red with blood. Thirty-six Apaches were killed. Forty others, hit by poisoned arrows, hid in the thick vegetation, only to exhale their life breath for the last time a short while later.

The Pimas gathered around Coro to touch his arms. Cegia, who had led the assault, rallied the warriors around their heroic chief. "We have a common soul now, we are one nation again. Your strength is in us. From now on, you lead us, and we'll win."

In three days, Quiburi gathered nearly all its inhabitants, and a week later, an all-out effort had succeeded in rebuilding close to two-thirds of the burned dwellings. Chief Coro passed the word out, "No work tonight. Tonight we celebrate our victory."

At the center of the village, six tall poles stood in a circle. Six leather thongs hung from each pole, each with a scalp attached. Just at sunset, a bonfire was lit and everybody gathered around to eat and drink. Then the drums started to beat, the rattles rasped, the flutes screeched, and the dance began. Women and children stood outside the circle of the poles, and the warriors who had triumphed over the Apaches ran inside the circle and slowly danced around each pole with measured steps. The drums beat faster, and the warriors jumped higher and higher. Then, at a signal, the rest of the warriors and the women ran to join the dance. Each woman chose a warrior and the dance became frenetic. Then Chief Coro stepped in the midst of the dancers and the drums fell silent.

"I have great news," he announced after quieting the crowd. "Not only we celebrate our glorious victory, but a new delegation of friends has arrived. The missionary Kino and a small army of his friends are here."

The circle widened, and Kino, Lieutenant Manje, Captain Bernal, and fifty cavalrymen were welcomed to the center. Coro called for silence. He asked the drums to beat softly at the tempo he indicated, and he began to sing. He sang of the sadness of losing the village, he sang about the pursuit of the Apaches. He sang of the hand-to-hand combat with Achak. He sang of the attack led by Cegia, and the final victory. His voice rose to high notes only a tenor could reach, yet could sink to depths that would challenge a bass. He sang of the common soul they had rediscovered, of the new unity it produced in the Pimas. He sang about the courage of his warriors, and the valor of the enemy. He sang of the faithfulness of his friends who came tonight. After he was done, he invited Kino to sing. "Sing to us of something that makes you great."

Kino, surprised, looked at Manje, but he looked away. He looked at Captain Bernal, who refused with a small wave of the hand. So Kino walked up to Coro, cleared his throat, and began his favorite chant—the Introit for the Easter Sunday mass. He chose the same tempo Coro had used. "Resu-u-rexi-i-i-i-i..." The drums joined in softly after the first few notes. "E-et adhuc te-e-cum su-u-u-u-um..." he continued. Coro's face lit up and he joined in a low ululation, "U-u-u-u, u-a-u-a..." improvising around Kino's singing, and with the slow dong-dong of the drums, it almost sounded like an organ playing.

Kino got to the end of the phrase and stopped, not wishing to push his luck. Coro, beaming, came to bear hug him. "What is it you sang? That wasn't Spanish."

"No, it is Latin."

"What does it say?"

"I am resurrected, and now I am with you forever."

"Teach me that, Kino! We too, we were like dead. This victory gave us new life."

The drums took up their fast beat, and the dance resumed. Women ran to the Spanish soldiers to dance with them. The soldiers hesitated, they looked at Captain Bernal. He hesitated and looked at Kino. The missionary clapped his hands with the beat, indicating they should dance. A woman came to him, but Kino deftly pushed her in front of Manje, who started to dance with her. Kino retreated to the outer perimeter of the dance.

After a while, Captain Bernal drew near him. "Thank you for singing. I'm not a singer, and I couldn't think of anything, my mind went blank. That was gutsy, singing a song from the mass. Coro loved it. I'm surprised you let the men dance."

"Why not? This dance is necessary—a scalp dance!"

"I think the scalps are a bit gory."

"Not for this occasion. This dance respects the dead. Each dancer comes face-to-face with his own mortality. Both sides lost men in the battle. It could have been anyone of the dancers."

"They're the lucky ones—the ones that stayed alive."

"True, that's a mystery—why me and not another? Still, what is essential is the transformation the battle worked in them. That's what is replayed now in the dance. Our mortality opens us to the thought of immortality, the thought that we're responsible for everything we do because we are watched over by a Providence that prepared everything for us as a favor, a celestial favor. How we execute it is our responsibility. That's why they must dance—to relive that experience as it first happened, to remember they live because others did not hesitate to die. Their sacrifice made it possible. Pimas are united by the courage of Coro, by the deaths of their own, even by the deaths of their enemies. Nothing is due to luck, everything is a favor."

"Do you mean it was better for them that we couldn't get here in time to help them defeat the Apaches?"

"Our slowness in getting here was part of the plan for their victory. The greatest victory is making good spring up from the defeat of evil. And this time, the victory is theirs alone."

Coro stomped up to Kino again. "Your song, Kino, still resounds in my ears. You also know that true life, and freedom, come from death and sacrifice? I believed that only we, Pimas, could grasp such truths."

"We don't only teach farming and cultivation at our missions. We teach how to live and die. We have a great master that taught us that."

"Then let's talk about that tomorrow, Kino. Let's decide when you will bring that master's teaching to us. But tonight, we dance."

Chapter 11

Manuel lifted his glass of beer and announced, "A toast, with deep sympathy for our past, and apprehension for an uncertain future. Maybe we should be singing a Requiem."

Hank and Roger joined him, lifting their wine glasses.

"Here's to a bright future for both of you," countered Roger.

"Do you see a silver lining to our tale of woes?" inquired Hank.

"No, but I expect the best is yet to come for you."

"Expect the best, and prepare for the worst, right?" suggested Manuel.

The waiter wound his way toward them around tables buzzing with conversations and restrained laughter, through a pleasant aroma of grilled meat and fish, carrying a large plate above his head. He set bread and a dish of tapenade on the table, then proceeded to list the special dishes on the menu of the day.

It was a mild winter evening. The sun had set, and gas heaters provided additional warmth to the diners seated outside, on the patio. Over the roofs of the shops on the east side of the plaza, through the branches of a tall sycamore tree, an orange moon, two days past full, was rising.

"How can any good come out of the situations Hank and I

are in?" continued Manuel.

"It will depend on you, I believe. Can you endure the wait, or will you give up before the events produce fruit?"

"Rodrigo and I will be canned fruit very soon, if the cartels decide to deal with us. Time is something we're short of. Why wait?"

"Because you don't know what to do. Now that you got rid of the drugs, you can't bargain. It wouldn't have worked anyway... You need outside help. I mean celestial favors." Roger smiled at Manuel.

"Yeah! Time for a Requiem."

"That can wait. It's time for expecting the good to start coming out of those events. You're in a potential well where you can be helped. Stay there until help shows up."

When Manuel nodded slowly, Hank turned to Roger and asked, "What's *my* potential well?"

"From what you told me, it's a very muddy situation. Your wife left because she couldn't wait for a change anymore. Then Pilar clarified the situation further. She made it clear that you should forget the past, and not repeat your mistakes. You need to be patient."

"My wife is impatient. She wants a divorce. But we will have an attempt at reconciliation before we go to court. She is coming to town with Celine and we will try one more time to work things out. That should happen in a few days."

"I believe things change when conditions are ready for the celestial favors to work," Roger said steadily.

"How can you tell it is ready?"

"When something unexpected happens and you have to make a choice. You are being tested. There is always a delay for a test. It's your choice to make. A choice between believing in Providence and the good it brings, or in randomness that brings nothing but despair, in the end. All life, all goodness, comes out of a potential well where it is prepared until it is time for its birth. Think about it this way: how long did it take to prepare intelligent life to appear on earth?"

"Oh... about four billion years, roughly. That's the latest number."

"Well, tell us about it," teased Manuel. Hank was happy to launch into an explanation.

"The evidence shows that we live in a rather safe zone in our galaxy, far away from disintegrating stars that would bombard us with deadly radiation. We're at the mercy of immediate annihilation, but we're remarkably protected by the extraordinary placement we enjoy in the galaxy, the extraordinary stability of our sun. We can also be thankful for the extraordinary presence of a magnetosphere around us to shield us from low doses of radiation. What should also make us think seriously about what Roger calls potential wells is the fact that life on earth is surprisingly protected by the presence of the moon. The moon's role in stabilizing the earth's obliquity for billions of years is well known."

"What do you mean by that?" asked Manuel.

The waiter showed up with the salads they had ordered. "Anything else I can bring you right now?" Everybody seemed satisfied. They wished each other *bon appétit*.

Hank continued, "The angle between the axis of spin of the earth and the plane of the orbit as it goes around the sun has a tiny wobble, but as compared to that of Mars, Venus, or Mercury, it is rock steady. If the earth's obliquity varied as much as that of Mars, the angle could have changed drastically, and the climate of the earth would vary so much that sustained animal life could not happen."

"Well, what's unique about the moon's role in this?" inquired Manuel.

"It had a pretty turbulent past. When men landed on the moon during the Apollo program and brought back quantities of rocks, the analysis of the lunar rocks revealed some amazing things."

"What amazing things?" Manuel probed further.

"The results were stunning," Hank continued, shaking his head. "The formation of the earth can be explained as a near collision with the moon. A body about the size of Mars hits the earth so that the two bodies, after a glancing blow, separate without pulverizing each other. In the process, the two bodies exchange materials. The earth steals the heavy metallic core, and the body that would become our moon captures some of the lighter outer mantle of the earth. The moon was located at only about fifteen thousand miles from the earth."

"That must have been a sight!" exclaimed Roger.

"The moon captured the material ejected and spiraling outward. If the moon had been orbiting in the opposite direction before the hit, it would have eventually collided with the earth. The earth's gain of heavy core metals gave rise to plate tectonics and a strong magnetic field. Without the moon, the tilt angle of the earth's spin axis with respect to the plane of its orbit would feel the effects of gravitational pull of the sun and Jupiter. As it is, the moon damps out those stressors. The climate of the earth would suffer extreme changes, and life would be impossible without this effect. The moon came at exactly the right time, the right angle, had the right size, and orbited in the right direction. Such an incredibly rare event is remarkable."

"Would you say it happened by design?" probed Roger.

"All I can say is that it created an exceptionally rare potential well for sustained life," admitted Hank.

"Rare? Why?" broke in Manuel.

"Life introduced in the zone near the earth-moon tandem has a chance to survive, not decay and die, like life on Mars apparently did. We should be grateful for that lifeless moon, our exceptional super-sized satellite," suggested Hank, looking back over his shoulder at the earth's silent companion, which had cleared the top of the sycamore tree. "Our good life today was prepared for us as a result of a catastrophic event that happened some four billion years ago. Our moon spilled its guts, so to speak, to bring about a potential well for life on earth. The proto moon was sacrificed for the sake of the proto earth."

"That's quite an example of a potential well!" exclaimed Roger. "Even today, we leave it at our own risk. It's extremely costly to live outside its boundaries. The slightest mistake can prove to be deadly."

"I know what you're suggesting," grumbled Hank. "Manuel and I should stay put until we receive a clear sign of what to do next."

Dinner was over. Hank insisted on picking up the tab. They stayed outside the restaurant for a while and looked up at the sky. The night was pleasantly cool. Orion was visible even through the brightness of the moonlit sky. They said goodbye, shook hands, and walked to their cars.

A few minutes later, Hank was home. He walked to the mailbox. A gentle breeze descended from the heights of Finger Rock, on top of the Catalinas, bright in the moonlight. A finger pointed at the sky.

There was a letter in the mail from Kim's lawyer. It made him feel as if a huge boulder was rolling down the mountain to crush him. He put it on top of the other mail. He glanced at Finger Rock again. How was he going to get that patience he needed to wait?

Chapter 12

"Padre Eusebio, dinner is ready, come and eat!" called Father Luis Velarde, his companion missionary at Nuestra Señora de los Dolores for the past eight years.

Kino got up and walked over to the ramada where the evening meal was served now that the daily temperatures were starting to climb. Luis thanked God for the gift of food they were going to eat, and filled Kino's bowl with his favorite squash soup. "Eusebio, this is an anniversary for you, isn't it? How long has it been? Twenty years?"

"I arrived twenty-four years ago today."

Time had flown by fast for the man of action, now sixty-six years old. He had been at Dolores twenty-four years. Twenty-four years protecting his Pimas from forced labor in the mines. His famous piece of paper granting immunity for twenty years was useless now. What protected his converts was the fame and reputation of the founder of the mission of Dolores.

Springtime was here again. Wildflowers covered the fields once more. The harvest was going to be abundant. He thought back to the early days of exploration of the Pimeria, the first chapels and farms built in the wilderness, the days he discovered, peering across the water of the gulf to the desert land of Baja California, that California was not an island. Manje had been a friend then. Manje, now a General, was a mine owner, and was asking the authorities for permission to use Pimas and Opatas for slave labor. He even spread rumors about the missionaries—how they refused to serve the settlers and favored the Pimas. Chief Soba had been right about his former friend. Kino thought gratefully about those who had helped him. Chief Coxi in Dolores, Chief Coro, the hero of the Apache frontier along the San Pedro, Chief Humari, east of the Santa Catalina mountains, those at San Xavier del Bac, and the Yumas on the Colorado River. What men of faith they had become, with simple hearts devoted to the truth.

"What is the biggest change you have seen in all those years?" Luis asked, trying to bring him out of his reverie.

"Oh, I've seen so many. Enemies became friends, and friends became enemies. But the biggest change is what is happening right now."

"What is that?"

"I never feared unknown tribes to the north, not even Apaches. I experienced hunger and thirst on long treks in the desert. I suffered from heat, even snow a couple of times. What I dread is the extinction, in men's souls, of the ability to recognize celestial favors, and ignorance of the responsibility they have to pass them on. That would defeat all the progress we made and stop us in our tracks. There would be no missions north of San Xavier del Bac."

"How far beyond San Xavier del Bac do you think we can extend our missions?

"I wrote the King several times to encourage him to send us boldly to California, to the lands way beyond Apacheria. I told him not to worry about expense. We would supply all our needs ourselves. He did not understand. He thinks he has to send troops and administrators, and he is looking for gold and silver to finance it."

Luis smiled at the bravado of the old vaquero, daring to tell a king how to run a kingdom, and his superiors how to organize the missions.

"But it takes such resources! People say we drain the wealth of New Spain. We're going too far, too fast. We're stealing resources that belong to the settlers and waste them on cultivating desert lands where so few souls live."

"There can be an Upper California to the northwest," Kino continued, "a New Navarre to the north, extending perhaps as far as New France, where other missionaries of our order are working. You ask where we should stop. We do not stop until all this New World has been raised by the leaven of Providence. Let's go north, let's join with those who do the same work we do and are coming south. Join as coworkers building the City of God. And the resources? That's not what is going to stop us. Nothing from the outside can stop us. What can stop us is from the inside, it is ourselves. The moment we receive a celestial favor, and think it is for our own use, that we have no responsibility to pass it on, we have begun to contradict the work of Providence. If, as a nation, we think we have done enough and should put the favors we have received in a vault or bury them in the ground, we have betrayed Providence. The moment you stop passing your gifts to others, they rot. And even worse, if you stop trusting in Providence, others stop trusting also. It's contagious. The whole nation rots. Eventually the nation will pass laws forbidding anybody to trust in it. Then the nation will collapse. People will flee, looking for places where they can trust again. What if one day there is no place, here or up north in the wilderness, where trusting in Providence is allowed anymore? That would be a catastrophe."

"What happens then?"

"I don't know, but what I know for sure is that out of great catastrophes, greater favors emerge. All it takes is for somebody, somewhere, to receive them and pass them on, and they will spread like wildfire in the desert."

"So many missions have been destroyed by the fires of rebellions. Why not slow down and regroup our forces?"

"The real rebellion, Luis, is not in the fields of our missions, it is quietly developing behind us, in the chambers of the Viceroy. He received all these gifts, people, land, a whole world open to the north, and he chooses to enjoy them for himself, and for the King. Watch how everything will rot. Nations all around shall see darkness and suffering. The world, man, and God form a choir. They sing together and there is peace. The desert itself blooms in the presence of that choir. Break up the choir and that reality disappears. The desert becomes hostile to man, and man to God. The choir needs to be formed again. If it is reunited, a small flame is ignited in the heart of man. The flame burns the rotten saguaros and chollas in the desert. When the choir sings again, a wildfire burns the deadwood of the nations. It produces fresh growth. It gives back to men the joy of their youth. Lands, kingdoms, nations are a gift that should be acknowledged as in a chant. Will the people in the future be able to recognize the celestial favors offered? Will they receive them and pass them on? Or will they just let them rot?"

Next day Kino was in the saddle, his little pack safely attached behind him. As always when he was going to ride alone in the desert, he could not repress a smile. He was going to Magdalena to officiate at the dedication of a chapel in honor of San Francisco Xavier. He was going to visit his old friend, Father Augustin De Campos, in charge of the Magdalena mission. The ride from Dolores to Magdalena was only a short warm-up for Kino, the long distance rider.

Luis Velarde was standing in the courtyard watching him

get ready to leave.

"Eusebio, is there anything I can do for you while you are gone?"

"Certainly. Pray for me. And now, give me your blessing."

"With pleasure, Eusebio."

Luis took the crucifix from around his neck and blessed his beloved superior with it.

"Come back quickly. I need you here."

"Amen!" Kino agreed. "Until we meet again!"

The mass had just started. Kino was standing at the foot of the steps leading to the altar and Campos was kneeling next to him. Kino was leading the prayers.

"Send your light and your truth, O God, they will be my guides toward your holy dwelling and your tabernacles."

"And I will enter the altar of God, the God who replenishes the joy of my youth," Campos responded.

"I will praise you with a harp, O God, my God. Why are you sad my soul, why do you make me sigh?"

"Put your hope in God. I will praise him again, my God, you, the salvation of my countenance."

"Glory be to the Father, the Son and the Holy Spirit."

"As it was in the beginning, so now and for all centuries of centuries. Amen."

Then Kino said very slowly,

"I will enter the altar of God."

Campos answered, "Of God who replenishes the joy of my youth."

Campos looked up at Kino, who seemed to be lost in thought. Campos reflected with a hint of a smile that he must be getting old. He waited a few seconds.

Kino, meanwhile, was with his favorite saint, San Francisco Xavier. "Do you remember when you were sick in Hall, near Innsbruck?" the saint asked.

"Yes," whispered Kino. "I prayed for you to ask God to help me so I could live longer, to be a missionary like you."

"You were given a favor, then. You used your favor wisely. It is time for you to enter the tabernacles of God at the center of the City of God."

"The tabernacle of the God who replenishes the joy of my youth..." Kino looked at his favorite saint with admiration. "You look young, Francisco Xavier."

"You too, Eusebio. You were never able to teach people what to call you, could you? Francisco Xavier, Eusebio, Chini, Kino?"

"I gave up when they couldn't remember if I was Italian or German."

"The important thing is that you trustingly passed on the favors you received."

"Will I get more favors?"

"Luis is able to continue with the favors you got. He will distribute them. But you, you will get your greatest favor yet."

"My greatest?"

"You are offered to give up all the favors you received in exchange for one that you cannot even think of. Are you ready?"

"With the help of Nuestra Señora de los Dolores, I am."

Suddenly Kino's legs weakened, and he fell to his knees on the lowest step of the altar.

"Eusebio! What's wrong?" asked Campos.

Kino could hear, but he said nothing. Campos grabbed him and dragged him back to the sacristy.

"Eusebio? Are you sick? Can you continue with the mass?"

Kino shook his head.

"Do you want to lie down and rest?"

Kino indicated with his head that was what he wanted. Campos picked him up and, with the help of two Pimas who had come into the sacristy, carried him into an adjacent room where Kino's belongings were. They laid him on his horse blanket, directly on the ground.

Kino looked at his saddle and leaned his head toward it. Campos pulled the saddle close and propped his friend's head on it.

Campos left to take over the mass. He turned in the doorway to look back, reluctant to leave his friend.

Kino was alone. All had left, including Francisco Xavier. He felt a cold weakness invade him. He could neither see nor hear, but his will and understanding were unchanged. This utter inability to do anything scared him. He thought death was like blowing out a candle. The light goes out, and the peace of sleep follows. This was different—total lack of sense perception, but an alert will and intellect. He was going along a straight path set out for him long ago. He could only accept it, or reject it. His whole past was available for review. He started remembering all he had done, and it made him uneasy. It was a long list of sins. So he stopped and let the darkness enter him. It came with a great pain, a total abandon into something he could not name. Then his will sensed a flicker of light. He willed to follow the light and a cry came to him.

"My God, My God, why have you abandoned me?"

Then, far away, a sort of grayness dawned. A certain understanding came close to him, and he agreed to it.

"Lord, take and receive my whole being. Take my memory."

As he said that, the list of sins was gone, he could not remember anything except who he was, and who he wanted to be. His past became indifferent. In front of him there was only a path to the source of Providence, barely visible, but straight and level.

"Lord, take my understanding."

He could not reason on anything anymore but on the hope of getting to the end of the path he was following and the light toward which it led.

"Lord, take my will and my liberty."

The path became wider and it seemed to be shortened. Nothing could be changed anymore.

"Lord, give me your grace and your love. That's all I want."

All things near him disappeared, even the presence of that first understanding. The cold weakness left, grayness became brightness, and happiness invaded him. He was flying toward the entrance of the tabernacle, the tabernacle of God who replenished the joy of his youth.

Chapter 13

Miguel woke before sunrise to make coffee. He was much improved. Four days of rest had reduced the swelling by half, and now he could hobble if he did not put his full weight on the knee. He could move across the room without crutches. He spent his days indoors to avoid the inquisitive eyes of police and Border Patrol. At night he went outside to observe the majestic procession of the stars and be filled with the silence of the desert. His business in Colorado should have been finished by the end of this day. He had promised his wife, Dolores Christina, that he would call after a week, before starting his journey home. He longed to get moving again.

Awakened by the aroma of the percolating coffee pot, Manuel dragged himself out of bed.

"That smells good. How about eggs and bacon to go with your coffee, Miguel?"

"Que bueno!"

He waited a moment before continuing, "Manuel, the less I impose on your hospitality, the better for all of us. I have to call my wife to tell her what happened, so she doesn't worry. I would like to call her today. After that, I can return home. My knee is better, much better."

"Whoa! Hold it Miguel! You can move like a coyote that's

lost a leg in a trap, but as for running back all the way you came, that's going to take a few more days."

"I can stand on both legs. I can walk. I'm not risking getting you involved in my problems any longer, Manuel."

"Oh yeah? And if they catch you going back, you're gonna tell them what?"

"I'll make sure nobody catches me, hombre."

"One thing at a time, Miguel. Let's call your wife. But not from here."

"Where from?"

"Roger's place. Here we are watched, and you never know who's listening." He rummaged for a few seconds in the kitchen drawer to find a piece of paper. "Give me the number to call for your wife."

"You two are up early," sighed Rodrigo, coming into the kitchen and positioning himself near the stove.

"Good timing, sobrino! We need a cook. You're elected. Make eggs and bacon for everybody. I'll run down to Robles Junction and be right back."

He grabbed Miguel's phone number and was gone before Rodrigo could figure out what happened.

The dawn was hesitating on the east side of the mountain as he dropped into the valley. He arrived at the gas station at Robles Junction, put some gas in the tank and entered the store. Ten minutes later, he came out, jumped in the car, and hightailed back home for breakfast.

As Manuel's car sped away, a white and green Border Patrol SUV pulled into the gas station. Two men stepped out, carefully looked around, and entered the store. They went to the back aisle and waited for the lone customer to get his change and leave. They approached the clerk. "Do you know the man who came in before the one that just left?”

“Manuel? Sure do!”

“What did he want?”

“Nothing. He paid for gas.”

“That’s all? Are you sure?”

“He made a phone call from the back office.”

“You know who he called?”

“I have no idea. He is a friend. I didn’t ask.”

“Does he call from here often?”

“No, never does.”

“So why now?”

“I didn’t ask.”

“Where did he call?”

“I didn’t ask.”

“You don’t ask much, do you?”

“I ask friends all there is to ask about. The rest is their business.”

“All right then, friend, have a good day. Thanks!”

“No problem.”

Later that same afternoon, Manuel and Roger met at the administration building at Kitt Peak.

“Did you contact Miguel’s wife, Dolores?” asked Manuel.

“Yes, I did,” said Roger.

“What did she say?”

“She was worried and asked a million questions I couldn’t answer. Then she said she is coming to see me here, at my house. She is driving to Tucson. She wants to see Miguel. She is arriving the day after tomorrow. I tried to tell her to wait, but nothing doing. She begged me to let her come. So you have to bring Miguel to my house. Bring Rodrigo also, she wants to meet everybody. You can all stay."

"Gracias! Wow! She makes fast tracks, that woman. Wait a minute. She doesn't have crazy ideas about driving back with him, does she?"

"No. She knows he's got to go back he way he came—on foot. She wants to come to talk to him and help him decide when to get back home."

"How did you speak to her?"

"My wife called first. She speaks some Spanish. But it turns out Dolores is fluent in English, so Francesca gave me the phone and we chatted."

"Thanks for calling her, Roger. We will be at your house the day after tomorrow. We'll be there in the morning."

"Be careful, Manuel. Hank told me that ICE is interested in your guest."

"I'm not surprised. We're watched. Maybe they know about Miguel."

"Should we invite Hank?"

"OK, invite him."

"Everybody's coming, maybe we should also invite ICE?" joked Roger.

"No thanks. Some other time."

Two days later, after hiding Miguel's crutches under a tarp in the truck bed, Manuel got into his pickup truck and called his two partners. Rodrigo jumped in next to him, in the middle, and Miguel sat on the right side. Manuel drove down into the valley and turned onto Ajo Highway, toward Tucson.

"No matter what happens, Miguel," said Manuel, "you stay seated where you are, and don't get excited."

"You don't want me to pretend I don't speak English?"

"Not a good idea," laughed Manuel.

"Let's hope nobody sees us," said Rodrigo.

The truck was approaching the eastern limit of the Tohono O'odham land. It crossed a cattle guard, dipped in a dry wash and hopped back up on a small rise.

"Do these washes ever get flooded in this desert?" asked Miguel.

Before anybody could answer, coming immediately after a right turn, they saw a white and green car and a van of the same colors parked on the right shoulder, and a Tohono O'odham police car parked a bit further ahead.

"Here we go! La Migra and the police! Keep cool!"

An agent of the law stepped on the road in front of them and motioned them to stop behind the parked vehicles.

"We are wanted," sighed Manuel as he pulled over.

"Good morning, gentlemen," said the lawman. "May I see your identifications?"

The three took their driver licenses out of their wallets. Manuel and Rodrigo gave theirs to Miguel who handed them to the agent.

"Thank you." He disappeared in the van. About five minutes later, the man came back.

"Here you are. Thanks. Have a good day." He handed the licenses back to Miguel.

Manuel pulled out slowly onto the road and drove off.

"Well, that was easy," remarked Rodrigo.

"So far, so good," agreed Miguel.

"Yeah! It's not bad, but not perfect either," mused Manuel.

"What do you mean?" asked Rodrigo.

"You didn't see the car parked in front of the van?"

"The police car?"

"Yes. You saw the men sitting inside? Cesar and Paulo! Those two are up to something. I wouldn't be surprised if they were expecting us and asked La Migra to set up the control."

"How would they know we were coming?"

"I don't know. Just a hunch I have. Why are they huddling with fellas from La Migra?"

"You're too suspicious," said Rodrigo.

"I hope you're right, Rodrigo. After all, it's for you they salivate."

"Thanks for the reminder."

After a fifty minute uneventful drive, Manuel turned onto a dead-end street and pulled up to a gate flanked by a mailbox decorated with painted butterflies. He opened the gate, pulled inside on the steeply inclined driveway, closed the gate behind him, and drove up to the house. At the top of the hill, the driveway circled in front of a house with a low white stucco wall and a loggia running along its west side. Between the driveway and loggia, a patio led to a small pond, and beyond it, a garden. The Catalinas to the north and Rincons to the east walled in a vista of rolling hills interspersed with horse ranches and pecan orchards. Mesquite and paloverdes competed with south facing stands of saguaros.

Miguel slid carefully out and leaned against the fender to test his knee's strength. Rodrigo grabbed the crutches from under the tarp. As they looked around for the door hidden under the loggia, a cat moseyed toward them and sat down at a safe distance. Suddenly, the door flew open and Dolores ran toward Miguel. Francesca and Roger followed close behind. Miguel almost lost his balance trying to embrace his wife.

"You can stand up! You don't look too bad, Miguel," cried out Dolores. "I was so worried."

"I got a lot of rest and stayed with good company. Dolores,

this is Manuel."

Dolores was a small woman, under five feet, with jet black hair, dark eyes, a light complexion, prominent cheekbones, and a slightly aquiline nose that gave her a strong determined look and made you forget her small stature. She looked up at the tall imposing Tohono O'odham holding her hand.

"Are you the one to thank for taking good care of my husband?"

"No señora, you should thank my sobrino, Rodrigo. He found your husband lying under a tree," said Manuel, letting go of her hand.

"Then I thank you, young man," she said. "You're the Good Samaritan who saved my wounded husband."

Rodrigo smiled shyly. "It was my good fortune to rescue him, señora."

"When did you get here?" asked Miguel.

"Early this morning. I got through customs in Nogales before the crowds."

"Any trouble getting through?"

"Nada! On our side, they barely looked at me. On the U.S. side, they were all business. Their drug-sniffing dog ran around the car without slowing down, and that was all. They gave me my passport back in less than five minutes."

"Let's go in," Francesca invited. "It's still chilly outside this morning."

Hank turned onto the dead-end street and stopped in front of the gate. As he closed the gate and drove up the hill, a black pickup truck turned slowly onto the street and parked a hundred yards from the gate, its engine running.

On top of the hill, Hank recognized Manuel's dusty white truck and parked behind it.

Roger and Francesca came out to greet him, followed by the rest of the group, except for the calico cat, who hesitated, arched her back, and hid behind the wolfberry bush.

The black pickup truck slowly came up to the gate. It stopped for a moment, then turned around and drove off.

An hour later, the discussion was going strong inside the house.

"My question," Manuel was saying, "is why there is such connivance by both sides to ignore illegal border crossing? Here Miguel was asked—officially, I must say—to enter illegally for a mission that could have been done above board, openly. It seems to me that both sides prefer to act in secret."

"I say both sides choose not to reveal their hand," affirmed Dolores. "Our two governments have a habit of ignoring each other. There has never been much love between them. Do to the other as you want, and hide your reasons—that's their game."

"You think so?" asked Francesca.

"Look at the difference with Canada. The U.S. deals with their northern neighbor as with a golf partner. Each one's move is discussed amiably and each congratulates the other for every stroke. With Mexico, it deals as with a hired gardener. Tell him what to do, pay the lowest wages, and check to make sure the gardening tools are still in the shed when he leaves. Mexico, in turn, looks at the northern neighbor as a usurper of territories who will not hesitate to take over huge chunks of Mexican lands, and as an unreliable trade partner, who will seize control of the raw resources of the country."

"Wait a minute!" exclaimed Manuel. "Who is taking over who? Aren't Mexicans infiltrating us at the rate of thousands every day, so that people are now saying Arizona will soon revert to Mexico?"

"Today, sure. But are you aware that the first wetbacks, as you call them, came from the north and they swam south?" Dolores shot back. "Migration started when Anglos began to come to the Mexican state of Texas, at first legally, then illegally, after Mexico closed the border in 1830. Anglos crossed the Rio de Sabinas from Louisiana and became illegal residents of Texas. Texas had to be combined with the state of Coahuila to try to dilute the illegal immigrant population into the larger Mexican population of that state. But that did not slow down anything, because the vast border could not be patrolled effectively. Doesn't that sound like today's news in reverse?"

Manuel was amazed. "Are you serious?"

"Check your history books!"

"That's right," Francesca jumped in. "The Sabine River, as it is called now, was the border between the U.S. and Mexico."

"But why does the attitude of ignoring each other persist today?" asked Roger.

"A lot of injustice is involved. History would reveal such a pile of dead bodies that both sides would rather bury the details. Injustice forgotten is injustice that never happened—that's what both governments pretend."

"Yet, that can't be true," cut in Roger. "Injustice is never forgotten. 'The voice of your brother's blood is crying to me from the ground' said God to Cain. No matter how deep they try to bury injustice, it will be unearthed someday. Maybe that's what's happening."

"What was the injustice?" Hank inquired.

"There were many, on both sides. But the biggest was what happened to our country under the regime of Plutarco Calles, in the early part of the twentieth century."

"What did he do?" questioned Manuel.

"He destroyed the soul of Mexico. He passed laws forcing

priests to register with the government to secularize them. He took over all religious buildings and Church property. This caused the Cristero rebellion in many states, a war that devastated our country for years."

"Why pass such laws?" wondered Francesca.

"To force people to turn exclusively to the State for all their needs, from health, to education, to the right to work, and the right to vote. Mexico had been a rich country, where most needs were provided by independent means, through the Church or benevolent organizations. Calles forced the people to be subservient to the State. Nobody else but the State was allowed to provide anything that the people needed. The Church stood in the way and had to be destroyed."

"Just as Kino had foreseen!" interjected Roger. "The State had to become the only provider to the nation. Providence had to be discredited."

"You know about Padre Kino?" remarked Miguel.

"We have a statue of him in town," answered Hank.

"Roger and I have been talking about him a lot, lately," explained Manuel. "He kept saying that everything, good or bad, is a celestial favor. Bad things work out for the good of those who trust in Providence."

"The three of us, Manuel, Roger, and I, have formed a choir —an organization to help us see Providence behind all events. Would that be outlawed in Mexico?" mused Hank.

"Under Calles' regime, you would have been shot," retorted Miguel.

"But don't fool yourselves, today in your country, you can see the same plan being implemented into law," warned Dolores. "It starts with health and education, continues with the right to work, and if not stopped, ends with any form of religion being forbidden."

"All the people fleeing Mexico today, hoping to find a better place to raise a family are doing it in vain?" asked Francesca.

"Probably. Our country has lost its soul. It has been ruled by one party for too long. If you follow the same trend, you will be like us. Religion is not forbidden anymore, as it was under President Plutarco Calles, but the damage is done, and our new presidents don't dare undo it. Providence is far behind the State in the minds of people. The Church is only their insurance policy for things beyond death, just in case they might exist."

"So why do they keep coming?" continued Francesca.

"They can make more money here," explained Miguel. "And there are some advantages in your country. You haven't disintegrated as much as we have, I suppose."

"There's maybe another reason," added Roger. "Interpreting events as Kino taught us, there's a favor for us in this exodus through the desert. Each disintegrated family unit walking through the desert brings a message to us, if only we would listen. It says take a good look at what happens to a nation when it surrenders its conscience to a State that forbids trust in Providence and erects itself as the only providence. The people crossing the desert say: learn from us. If you do nothing, it will happen to you. But are we listening?"

"What can we do to prevent this from happening here?" asked Francesca.

"According to Kino, everything is a favor," explained Roger. "The gift of independence from an oppressive government that was given to us must be passed on to Mexico. And Mexico's lesson, paid in blood, and suffering, and endurance, must be told everywhere. It must not be hidden."

"Very true!" exclaimed Dolores. "Our government is pretending that Calles and the Cristero rebellion never happened. The truth is hidden or distorted. A government that lies and distorts the truth is a failed one. Such a government never recognizes responsibility for failures. It just rewrites history."

"But how can we fight against a propaganda of lies?" insisted Francesca.

"Kino said it starts with individuals. A few must regain the practice of trusting in Providence and pass the tradition on to others. He said it was contagious. A few souls can invigorate the soul of the nation. Providence works through individuals, and makes them pass from being citizens of the City of Men to citizenship in the City of God, agents of His Providence. They become the souls of the nation and bring it back to what it really is—one nation under God. It begins with a choice we make every day. Once started, it propagates through the whole nation."

Francesca looked at her watch. "Anybody hungry for lunch? Dolores and I will serve it. It will be ready in a few minutes."

They walked out into a cool breeze descending the broad shoulders of the Rincons. They walked to the pond and took in the view of the Catalinas. The patio overlooked a steep gully carved out by summer monsoon rains into a sandy path devoid of vegetation.

Rodrigo dropped down into the gully and walked about a hundred yards until it met the property's fence close to the entrance gate. He was climbing out of the gully onto the driveway when he saw a black pickup truck turn around in front of the gate and slowly drive away. He heard his name called. It was Francesca. Lunch was ready. He hurried back to the house.

Manuel walked into the dining room and noticed two paintings showing scenes from the life of Padre Kino, hanging on the wall. "I see you like Padre Kino, Francesca. Where did you get these paintings?"

"Here in town. They are not originals, of course, but we love them."

Miguel came up close, to admire them. "Ah! Our Padre Kino. I guess he is yours too, since he founded the Mission del Bac, outside of town."

Late in the afternoon, the group was still discussing the events in the life of Padre Kino and its impact on the formation of what used to be called Pimeria, now split between Sonora and Arizona, and its relevance to modern politics.

Francesca glanced at the window, looking out to the cars parked in the driveway. Cleo the calico cat had just jumped to the window sill, yellow eyes big with fear, mouth wide open in an alarming meow, urgently requesting attention. Francesca opened the door and Cleo ran in and disappeared into the master bedroom.

"Cleo! What got into you? Did you see a javelina?"

A yowl of indignation came out from the bedroom as an answer. Francesca stepped outside to look. The sun had set behind the ridge top, and shadows were accentuated by the backlit sky. She couldn't see anything clearly, and everything seemed as usual.

"I don't know what scared her. It's time for her afternoon snack anyway," commented Francesca as she rejoined the group.

Behind Manuel's truck a dark form had been kneeling, immobile, waiting for Francesca to go back inside. A man dressed in black crouched down and removed a small object from his coat pocket. He got flat on the ground, crawled under the rear differential, and felt carefully to find a good spot. He then stuck the tiny magnetized personal navigation device on the metal above the differential. He searched his pocket for the receiver, turned it on, and checked to read the position indicated on his own GPS display. After verifying that everything worked, he put it back in his pocket and wiggled out from under the truck. He carefully got up, checked the direction toward the door Francesca had opened, and scanned all azimuths around him. He could see nothing that shouldn't be there.

He let himself down into the gully Rodrigo had explored earlier, and got back into his black pickup truck. At the end of the street, he turned onto Speedway Boulevard and escaped toward the city.

"How long do we have to sing together before we get the courage to act on our convictions?" Manuel asked Roger.

"Nobody knows. When ready, you'll be given the occasion. Courage or not, it will be your time. All you have to do is accept the gift."

Chapter 14

A message crackled over the radio. "Suspected illegals, going north, five miles south of Topawa."

"Who spotted them?" asked Paulo.

"Spotted by UAV," came the answer.

"OK, got it," replied Paulo.

"Great! Those damned machines are flying again this week," grumbled Cesar. "Probably another false report. Last time they tagged some residents of Gu Vo as illegals. I hope it's not going to be another week like that. We wasted a whole afternoon looking before we realized they were wrong."

"From three thousand feet up, it's not easy to tell the difference between our own people and illegals."

"Then why use those machines? Trained pairs of local eyes are better than ten of those expensive doomsday machines. Why can't they hire some of our people and pay them?"

"That's progress, boss. You have to go with progress," replied Paulo. "We're guinea pigs here. The virtual fences near Sasabe and Ajo don't work. This area has become a superhighway for drug traffickers. So we're getting drones and all kinds of machines right over our heads. Now they've decided to load them with guns so they can shoot people if they want to."

"If they start doing that they might kill one of our own."

A cold wind was carrying fast moving clouds from the northwest. Baboquivari showed a dusting of snow on its head, and silvery filaments of snowmelt cascaded down waterfalls to fill arroyos tumbling down to the bajada.

"Another cold, windy day," complained Paulo. "I wish the wind would bring rain. That would be good for the flowers this spring."

"Never mind the flowers. You should be concerned about our future," grumbled Cesar. "We have to get control of this situation. Our jobs are at stake."

"You worry all the time. Nothing to do, except wait. Nobody knows a thing about our combo. Not a trace of the merchandise was found, so nobody can blame us. Chill out."

"Are you kidding me? Miguel sure found something, and El Pato, for sure, is missing something. That makes for a hell of a mess. These two get together and start yakking to the wrong people, and you and I are bound for a government-provided cabana in Yuma for the rest of our lives."

"Use your brain, Ceasar, and don't give ulcers to your stomach. Maybe we have to shake up things in our organization."

"I tell you, Paulo, this is a winning combo. It's like an anthill. Worker ants gather the merchandise, soldier ants supervise to see it's done right. You're lucky, muchacho, you're a soldier ant. You know the worker ants. But none of them knows you. Rodrigo, he doesn't know who he's working for. He picks up the merchandise from Sureño and delivers it to Del Norte, that's all."

"That's what I don't like about it. If he knew more, he wouldn't have been shook up when Sureño told him not to deliver to Del Norte but wait for the police at his house. He had no idea it was us. We were looking out for him.”

“No, I like it the way it is. Rodrigo doesn’t know a thing. It’s better for you and me. But that idiot Sureño should have put it another way. Not ‘the police’, but ‘friends in the police’. Something like that. He screwed up on that one!”

“That’s what you told him to say, right? ‘Don’t deliver to Del Norte, wait at your house for the police.’ Your anthill organization screwed things up.”

“That stupid Rodrigo! He’s got it easy. Pick up from one ant, deliver to another ant. No questions, no change, no worry. And the first time there is a change, what does he do? He panics, he disobeys, and worst of all, he goes to Manuel, that double-dealing smart burro. Now the merchandise is hidden and we can’t find it.”

“Maybe you shouldn’t have said anything and let the deal go through.”

“Not on your life! First of all, it was twice the weight agreed to. But most of all, it was not pot—it was part cocaine! You know how much that snow costs? You think I will deliver cocaine for the price of pot, so El Pato can get filthy rich, and me risk the pen for life?”

“I tell you, it would have been out of our hands. You wouldn’t sweat like a pig now.”

“You think I would let El Pato pull a fast one like this, and say nothing? I would rather see him rot in prison.”

“Yeah. And us with him, now that we’re involved.”

“We’re involved because of this two-timer Miguel. He comes and he thinks he can steal the merchandise and run. What are we? Some small-time pot peddlers? He thinks he is an untouchable drug lord? I’ll show him what kind of machos we are. I prefer to deal with that cheat, El Pato, any day. Miguel, he's got something coming to him, for sure."

"You don't know for sure about Miguel. Why do you refuse to talk straight with Rodrigo? You could learn what Miguel has to do with this mess."

"Paulo, sometimes I doubt you've got common sense. Think, Paulo, think! Rodrigo gives the merchandise to Manuel. Manuel hides it. A few days later this Miguel drops in out of nowhere. For what? Pay his respects to Manuel? Don't be stupid. They know they are sitting on a big deal. They want to give it to Miguel, who can take it out of their hands to Phoenix or Los Angeles and pay them enough money to retire. That's clear to me. There's no doubt."

"You don't know Manuel, that's all."

"I know his nephew Rodrigo. It's Miguel I can't stomach. He's screwing up our business and making it dicey for our freedom."

They were approaching the road that led to Manuel's house, high on top of the bajada.

"Pull in and park behind these trees," suggested Cesar. "From here, we can see for a good five miles."

"We can see everybody except Manuel and his guest Miguel. They're still in Tucson."

"And being watched by El Pato. He's not going to let his merchandise be stolen. You can count on that."

"Cesar, I tell you, you seem to trust El Pato more than Manuel. I wouldn't have given him the information about Miguel and where he was going with Manuel. He might make a mistake and get us in trouble."

"You don't understand, Paulo. I can't go and show myself around that house in Tucson, but El Pato can. It's your friend Tito from La Migra who gave you the information, and it was a very fortunate thing. This way, we can have somebody keep an eye on the whole gang while they have a meeting at this guy's house. What's his name?"

"You mean Roger?"

"Yeah, that's it. Roger."

"See, Cesar, that's another thing. I got the information from Tito as a favor. He told me who Manuel had called from Robles Junction. But nobody but us was supposed to know it. Now you gave it to El Pato. If he makes a mistake, La Migra could ask how El Pato knew where the meeting was. That's another involvement of both of us with him. I just don't trust this El Pato as far as I can spit."

"You're making things up. It's Miguel I don't trust."

"You trust El Pato who sent a threatening message to Rodrigo?"

"He didn't do anything to him, did he?"

"That's because he knew we're in the loop. Otherwise, he would have acted."

"OK. So you don't trust El Pato, and I don't trust Miguel. That's the way it should be. The less you trust, the less you can be caught. In today's world, you have to trust nobody."

"Great world we live in, Cesar!"

"It's not my fault, I didn't make it."

"Are you sure? You're contributing to it with your attitude."

"Don't get teary-eyed on me, Paulo. Where are those illegals? Are they coming?"

"Not yet, it's all quiet. Nobody here but us."

El Pato had been watching the GPS receiver, waiting to see movement from Manuel's tagged vehicle. He was getting tired of waiting, as a matter of fact. When it finally happened, it was nine in the morning, and his heart jumped. He watched the position change. It was going west on Irvington, south on Kolb. When it turned west on Valencia, he was sure Manuel's group was going home via Robles Junction. He called his right hand man immediately.

"Pascual? It's time. They're coming. Get ready. Wait for my call. I'll talk to you again when I get there."

"I have only five men today. That leaves me, on one side, with only two people."

"I need three on the east side. You'll have to do with two on the west side. Be careful. Nobody passes either direction when I tell you."

"Can do! No problem."

El Pato jumped in his black pickup truck and drove two blocks to Mario's house. Mario was waiting on the sidewalk with a small duffle bag. He put the bag on the floor in front of the passenger seat.

"Everything ready, like we planned, Mario?"

"Sure, boss."

El Pato drove west on Route 86, drove past Robles Junction and turned right into Fuller road. He made a U turn to face Ajo Road. He checked Manuel's position on the GPS. Manuel's truck was three miles east, coming towards them. He called Pascual.

"Pascual? It's time to stop traffic on the eastbound lanes."

A few seconds later, a quarter of a mile east of the Tohono O'odham border, two men put signs on the side of the road leading east toward Tucson, warning 'Roadwork ahead, Be prepared to stop'. They placed a few orange cones in the middle of the road. One man waited, holding a stop sign, and the other stood in the middle of the eastbound lane. Less than a minute later, a large camper pulling a trailer loaded with two motorcycles stopped at the signal, followed by three cars. The men politely smiled and waved reassuringly at the waiting traffic.

Meanwhile, El Pato saw Manuel's truck approaching in a file of five vehicles, three leading, and one trailing a bit. At a signal from El Pato, one man stepped in the middle of the road with a stop sign and made the last car stop. El Pato pulled out right behind Manuel's truck and followed. A short distance ahead, two other men with stop signs and cones let the first three cars pass and forcefully signaled for Manuel, followed by El Pato, to stop. One of the men approached Manuel, sitting with Rodrigo and Miguel next to him.

"Sorry folks, there's an accident ahead. They're cleaning up. It will take a few minutes."

Manuel waved his hand to show it was OK with him. A while later, the man came back and motioned Manuel and El Pato through. There were no cars behind them. Manuel accelerated, with El Pato on his tail. No traffic came from the opposite direction. They drove a mile, and suddenly El Pato pulled into the left lane, right in the middle of a right hand curve, ignoring the double yellow lines. In this area, for half a mile, the road passed between two buttes, one on each side of the road, hiding it from view from all directions. Manuel slowed down to let the truck pass, but the black pickup truck slowed down to stay parallel with Manuel. The dark tinted passenger side window rolled down, and Mario smiled benignly, then showed a pistol and waved it at Manuel.

Manuel floored the accelerator and his truck jumped ahead. El Pato did the same, caught up with him, and got slightly ahead. Manuel stepped on the brake and got just behind El Pato, with his front bumper almost touching the rear edge of El Pato's bumper. Then Manuel decided to go for it. He floored it again and hit the bumper while turning his steering wheel to the left. The bumpers grinded and the truck ahead made a clockwise sliding turn. For a second, El Pato and Mario faced Manuel, Rodrigo and Miguel, while the trucks kept moving. Manuel slammed on the brake to avoid hitting the black truck again. El Pato tried to correct the pivoting by steering to his right. His truck spun even faster and slid off the left side of the road, back end first, narrowly avoiding hitting a guard rail where the road passed over a gully. It side-slipped from the narrow shoulder to the bottom of the gully, where it hit some rocks and turned over on the driver's side. Manuel's truck kept going and disappeared behind the curve.

Mario emerged from a daze after a couple of minutes to find himself in a vertical position, with his feet pressing on El Pato's back. El Pato was slumped over at the bottom against the driver side door, motionless. Mario realized the truck was on its side and he had to get out. He climbed out of the passenger side window, which had shattered. He reached back and grabbed his duffle bag. The pistol was not in it. He climbed back in the truck and saw it had fallen right behind El Pato's neck. He shook El Pato.

"Pronto, amigo! Get out! Do you hear me?"

El Pato did not move. Mario stuffed his pistol under his belt, crawled out of the truck, hesitated a few seconds, and then took off on foot in the direction of Robles Junction. He stayed a safe distance from the road, hidden in the cover of creosote bushes and mesquite trees.

A few miles further west, Manuel came upon two men stopping the eastbound traffic. There were now about a dozen cars waiting. The two road workers looked in amazement at this lone truck approaching from the east where another roadblock was supposed to have prevented anybody from coming through. They realized something had not gone according to plan. As soon as Manuel passed them, they stepped aside and let the eastbound traffic flow again.

"There was no accident!" remarked Rodrigo.

"There's one now, back there," replied Manuel. "These guys are not road workers. This is a set up."

"What do these guys want?" asked Miguel.

"Maybe Rodrigo. Maybe you, Miguel. It was not a friendly chat they had in mind."

Cesar and Paulo were still in their car, waiting for illegals to materialize, when they received an emergency call.

"Accident about two miles east of the Tohono O'odham lands. Cesar, can you investigate?"

"Who called in the accident? Any witnesses?" asked Paulo.

"It was a 911 call. It's off the road, in a gully. No witnesses. Someone driving east saw the rollover and called 911. State police are asking if we can get there first. They've got no car close to there right now."

Paulo turned on his flashing lights and took off in a squeal of tires. As he entered Route 86, he turned on his siren and picked up speed. He was passing a line of cars when he had to slow down for a pickup truck turning across the road, heading south toward Ali Chukson. As soon as they passed it, Paulo resumed his breakneck speed.

"Well, well! Did you see that truck back there?" exclaimed Cesar.

"No. I was busy trying not to hit anybody."

"Our friends Manuel, Rodrigo, and Miguel are back!"

"Good! Now you can talk to Rodrigo about Miguel and square things off with them."

"Yeah... we'll see."

They saw a passenger car and a motorcycle parked on the

side of the road, with three people looking at the field below, and slowed down. As they pulled behind them, they caught sight of the overturned truck in the gully.

"Did you see it happen?" Cesar questioned the people at the scene.

"No, we were delayed for some time on account of the roadwork, and when we started moving, we got sight of this truck down there," explained the motorcycle rider.

"What roadwork?" asked Paulo.

"There's a crew back about a mile and a half, controlling traffic."

"Back there? A road crew?"

"Yes. They stopped us for several minutes. But there is a guy in that truck in the gully that needs immediate help. He seems in pain. We can't get him out. His truck is on its side and he is on the bottom, on the driver's side. You'll have to pull him out through the passenger side."

"Thanks folks. Stay here a minute. We'll take a look and we'll be right back."

Cesar and Paulo descended into the gully. They took a look around the truck and saw a man inside, moaning in pain.

"Damn! It's El Pato!" yelled Cesar.

"What? Are you sure?"

"Take a look. There's something fishy about this. There is no trace of the road crew, and yet the traffic was stopped. Here is El Pato, all banged up, and we just saw Miguel take off the other way. Smells like foul play. Who did it?"

"Manuel and Miguel don't know El Pato. Must have been planned by him. See Cesar, I told you not to trust him. We're in deep trouble."

"Not yet, amigo. Let's play carefully. We don't have to tell anybody about what we know. El Pato had an accident. That's all."

They climbed back up to the road. Two other cars stopped to look at the accident. Cesar told Paulo, "I'll take the names of the three guys we saw first. Then tell all to get the hell out of here. We don't need gawkers. Call an ambulance immediately, in case nobody sent one yet."

Cesar took the names, and the travelers left.

"What next?" asked Paulo.

"We wait for the state trooper. I can hear a siren. Take a look at the tire marks. It looks like El Pato did a one-eighty with his truck before exiting the road. I tell you, Paulo, we just saw Manuel and Miguel back there. I'm convinced now. Miguel's involved."

"Was he driving? Did you see back there?"

"No. It was Manuel. But they could have switched drivers. Apparently the traffic was controlled back where we came from. So be careful. Keep your mouth shut. I'll do the talking. Answer only if you are asked, and even then, let me do the explanations."

A minute later a state trooper joined them, made a U-turn and parked behind them.

"Is there an ambulance coming?" asked Cesar. "There's a man hurt down there."

"Yes, it will be here in a minute. And a tow truck is coming behind. Thanks for coming right away. I was in Avra valley when I got the call. I appreciate the help."

"That's the least we can do," answered Cesar. "Glad we can help. I have the names of three people who were here before us, in case you want to talk to them. They didn't see the accident, just reported it."

"Thanks, it might be useful. How did it happen?"

"No one saw it. That's how accidents happen around here.

It's a dangerous road and lots of people get killed. Mostly alcohol, you know."

"I know. This road is like a cemetery. Just look at all the roadside memorials."

"Right! And the worst is that most of them are our people," sighed Cesar.

"You're right."

The ambulance announced its coming with siren wailing. The paramedics and the lawmen went down to the truck. They talked to the man inside. The medics asked him questions and he managed to blurt out that he was hurt. While they tried to question him some more, the tow truck came. They made it turn back three hundred yards where the road was more level with the field next to the road. After bringing the tow truck close, they slowly pulled the pickup truck and righted its position to have better access to the man inside. After a few minutes El Pato, tied to a gurney, was carried to the ambulance, which took off, siren screaming, toward Tucson.

Cesar and Paulo stayed with the trooper and helped him measure tire marks and distances on the road. They exchanged business cards, shook hands, and drove off in opposite directions.

"El Pato saw you?" asked Cesar.

"No. I stayed behind the medics."

"Good, it's better this way."

"What do you want to do now?"

"Talk to Sureño."

"You're going to go all the way down to San Miguel?"

"Sure will. I want him to have the whole area from Baboquivari to the Mexican border watched day and night. I want to know about every jackrabbit that stirs in the area. I want to know when Miguel decides to make a move from

Manuel's house, in a car, on foot, or riding on a burro. I want to know his every step."

"You still have it in for him. You don't give up."

"I want to protect our hides, Paulo. If Miguel has to die, so be it."

"And what if El Pato is the one who squeals on us?"

"I am going to have him covered too. We are going to send Del Norte to investigate. I want to know exactly what happened to El Pato, who sent him to the hospital, and who organized that roadblock. Miguel and El Pato, both will have to deal with me."

Manuel parked his truck behind his house. The three occupants got out and hastened inside. Ten minutes later, they came out carrying flashlights, blankets, food, water, and all of Miguel's belongings, including his crutches. They walked rapidly and climbed to the mouth of the ringtail's cave. Half an hour later, Manuel and Rodrigo emerged, leaving Miguel hidden inside. They scouted the surroundings and made sure nobody had come up to the house. When they were sure, they quickly descended and reentered the house.

As evening drew near, Cesar and Paulo turned in their police car and went home. Just as he sat down for supper, Cesar's phone rang. It was Del Norte calling. He got up and walked to the bedroom and closed the door.

El Pato had been taken to the University Medical Center in Tucson. The news from the hospital was mixed. On the negative side, El Pato had a broken tibia, a dislocated shoulder, a sore neck, and maybe a slipped disc in his back requiring surgery. He was going to stay in the hospital for a few days. The good news was that he was being treated as a regular patient, not as a suspect. There was no suspicion of foul play or alcohol involved in the accident; the state trooper had only ticketed him for careless driving. Del Norte had no difficulty getting in to see him. There was no official mention of the road crew that supposedly had blocked traffic. The police either had no wind of it or were ignoring it. El Pato told Del Norte that he'd set up the roadblock because he wanted to kidnap Miguel and Rodrigo to force them to reveal the location of the merchandise. He had not counted on Manuel's expert driving. Manuel had sent him spinning off the road and he'd woken up in pain at the bottom of the gully.

El Pato was asking Cesar, as a favor, to take action against Miguel, whom he, El Pato, considered the mastermind behind this plot to defraud them of their merchandise. He was opposed to taking serious action against Rodrigo and Manuel, since they were locals and action against them would call the attention of outside agencies to the matter. His guess was the merchandise was gone from Manuel's house by now. El Pato was positive the merchandise was not taken to the Tucson address where Manuel had driven Miguel and Rodrigo. He had gone there himself, following a few minutes behind, arriving while they were still talking outside. Nothing was removed from the truck, and he had checked the truck himself. He was convinced Miguel already had the merchandise moved out for distribution. Miguel had to be punished. There was no other choice.

Cesar gave Del Norte an order for a tight surveillance of Manuel's house. No truck should leave without his knowing. Nobody, even on foot, should go unreported. "I am sure Miguel will leave very soon, now that he knows he's wanted," he told Del Norte, "so be more observant than a hungry vulture."

Del Norte assured him he had the whole area already watched. Nobody would move without being reported to Cesar.

The next morning, right after sunrise, Cesar received news that his prey had been spotted. Miguel was headed south, using a walking stick. He must have started in the dark because he was first detected at a place east of South Komelic, well on his way to the border. There was no time to waste.

Ten minutes later, Cesar and Paulo were driving toward the place where Miguel had been seen. They pulled onto the side of the road. Cesar took out binoculars and scanned the area.

The bajada extended to the steep slope of the Baboquivari Mountains. Mesquite, ocotillos, creosote and saguaros easily hid any human shape not wanting to be seen. He adjusted the binoculars and looked carefully at a flat area created by a large wash at the base of the bajada. Suddenly he spotted a human form, about two miles east of the road and half a mile south. The man was walking steadily but leaning on a stick and limping. "There's my target," Cesar whispered.

He must have injured a leg, Cesar thought. Good. That gave him a bit more time to plot. Here was Miguel, the man who'd stolen his merchandise, the source of all his problems. He was not going to capture him. He would make sure he got killed. Then he could force Rodrigo and Manuel to talk.

Cesar called his dispatching base. "Cesar here. Tell me, is there UAV surveillance today in our area?"

"There's supposed to be, but nothing reported yet. It should be there soon."

"OK, connect me with Border Patrol."

Cesar watched Miguel through the binoculars again.

"What do you intend to do?" asked Paulo.

"Let me do it. You just listen and stay quiet."

Three minutes later the dispatch called back. "Cesar? I have Border Patrol. It's Tito. I'll patch you in."

"Tito? Just the man I wanted to talk to. Tito, I have something interesting for you. I am one mile north of Topawa, and I am told a man is walking south toward the border. He is somewhere halfway between me and Cowlic. He is, so I am told, a drug lord, a key organizer of the traffic in this whole area. How would you like to help me arrest him?"

"He is walking south? Toward the border? That's a new one! Everyone else is walking north today."

"This guy, if you get him, could bring you a promotion. If what I was told is true, he is the biggest catch around here. How about it, Tito? Where're you now?"

"We are staked out near Big Field. Did you say Cowlic? I could be there in less than half an hour."

"Good, maybe you want to call for support."

"I can do that too. I'll take a look at this guy."

"I'll watch on this side and you take the other side. Between the two of us we can squeeze him. Stay in touch."

"OK."

"Thanks, Tito."

"What are you saying?" cut in Paulo as soon as Cesar finished. "You're giving him the wrong coordinates. Cowlic is a hundred and eighty degrees the wrong direction and miles away from where Miguel is going."

"Just trust me on this, Paulo. I want to get rid of Miguel once and for all. I don't want to capture him alive. He could talk too much. I have an idea how we can use all these new flying machines to our advantage. We're going to let him get closer to the border. We're going to force our friend Tito to send his flying machine to take out Miguel. When there's no alternative but that blasted UAV to stop Miguel, I'll call Tito and tell him who it is we want to stop. Tito checked his identity two days ago. He'll remember the name. That should be added incentive for sending the UAV to get rid of him.”

“Why kill him?” protested Paulo.

“Because you and I are involved. Dead, he cannot talk about us. I can make a deal with Manuel to keep him silent because of his nephew. He’ll want to protect Rodrigo. But Miguel must be silenced for good. He must die if we want to stay free.”

Miguel kept walking in the low areas of Baboquivari Valley about two miles east of the road from South Komelic to San Miguel. Whenever he judged he could be seen from the road, he descended in washes. When the road was hidden behind a rise or there was enough vegetation nearby, he came up to the valley floor to make better time. His knee was a bit stiff but did not bother him otherwise. He stopped every hour to drink water and take a few bites of some energy bars that Francesca had given him. He was making good time and figured he could be south of the border by mid-afternoon. The thought of Dolores waiting for him gave him strength to go on.

It had been an hour since Cesar talked to Tito. There was no communication from him yet. Cesar picked up his binoculars and, from his new observation post, soon found Miguel. He was now very near San Miguel, about five miles from the border, and still walking with his stick. He called Tito again. “Tito, I haven’t heard from you. What’s happening on your side?”

“Sorry Cesar, I didn’t go to find that man. I had to do ground verification for the UAV we have here. It’s an exercise. That’s top priority.”

“I was just calling you to change our plans. I was given wrong coordinates on the man I called you about. Our man is five miles from the border, and I can see him. If we don’t do anything he will just walk back into Mexico and we will never catch him. How would you like to do something real with your mechanical bird? What I propose to you is to intercept a real criminal, a drug lord, instead of playing at identifying targets on the ground. You can make your damn vulture fly over here and take out an enemy target. How about it?"

"How do you know he is a real target? I cannot risk making a mistake, you know."

"I can vouch for it. His name is Miguel Aguilar, the man whose identity was verified a few days ago going from our land to Tucson. You were there to do the control yourself, remember? Tito, this is a drug lord in charge of the traffic of cocaine through all of southern Arizona. I can see him. I am watching him through my binoculars right now."

Tito remained speechless for a few seconds, and then quickly, as if to cover up his hesitation, he said, "I remember the name. You're sure it's him?"

"Absolutely sure! Don't wait too long. He is very close to the border."

"I have to ask authorization to do it."

"Hurry then! Do it."

Five minutes later Tito called back.

"Well, what do you know? You're in luck! I got authorization to try to neutralize your man. The use of drones on drug traffickers has been approved now, so we can take action. Your guy will be the first one we try this on in this area. I'm sending the bird. Tell me exactly the location."

High above the bajada, just under the steep rise to the crest of Baboquivari, Rodrigo was watching out for Miguel. Manuel had suggested that Rodrigo accompany him, but Miguel had adamantly refused. He would be safer alone. Two people can be spotted easier, and he wanted to go back home unseen.

However, as soon as Miguel left, well before dawn, Rodrigo and Manuel agreed it would be good to keep an eye on Miguel's safety from a distance. Rodrigo packed water and food and took the high road, on the side of the mountain where he would be able to watch Miguel's progress.

At first he was alone in the dark, and could not see Miguel. When the sun rose, he caught sight of him immediately. Miguel was about three miles ahead, walking on a flatter trail, but his knee slowed him down slightly, and Rodrigo, on a steeper path zigzagging up and down, could easily keep up with him and remain out of sight. He saw Miguel stop occasionally to drink and have a snack. After Miguel had passed South Komelic, he caught sight of a police car driving south on the road. Miguel must have detected it also. He was invisible. The police car continued south. Miguel reappeared and Rodrigo resumed his walk on the high trail.

Miguel was now south of San Miguel. "He is home already! The place bears his name. The archangel will help him get home," smiled Rodrigo. He was glad the trek was coming to an end. It was two in the afternoon, and he could be back at Manuel's before midnight if he walked fast and in the open.

Miguel heard a noise coming from the west, a sort of hum at first, like a diesel truck, but at a higher pitch and quieter. He was emerging from a wash, close to a clump of mesquite trees. His reaction was to hide in the trees, so he laid low under the cover. About thirty seconds later, a drone flew by at some distance to the north and continued toward the mountains. It turned south, and then made a wide turn to the northwest. Miguel waited motionless, not knowing what the drone meant. The thing passed even further to the north this time, missing his hideaway by a quarter mile. Miguel looked up and saw it aim toward the top of the bajada. He was tempted to resume his walking home but fought the impulse.

Cesar saw the drone go beyond the point where he had seen Miguel. "Where's that stupid machine flying?" he yelled. "It's going the wrong way. There's nothing there!"

Rodrigo heard the buzz and searched for the source of the noise. Down below him somewhere, the sound of an engine could be heard. He thought it could be a powered hang glider, but as the sound became louder, he saw it. It was some kind of plane. Down below, Miguel had disappeared.

Rodrigo stopped to watch the drone. It was gaining altitude and apparently was coming straight at him. Realizing the imminent danger, he frantically searched for shelter. About a hundred feet ahead, there was a gully tumbling down toward the bajada. It was a good ten feet deep, more than enough to hide him. He reached the edge of the gully as the plane was closing in toward the mountain side, just at his altitude. He took one more look, lost his balance and rolled to the bottom of the gully just as a loud explosion hit the place where his feet had stumbled. Dirt and rocks tumbled down, completely covering him. He could not move, and all became dark.

Paulo had the binoculars aimed where the drone was flying, well away from where they suspected Miguel was. He saw the drone fire a small rocket and a geyser of dirt rise from the impact.

"What did they do?" asked Cesar.

Tito's voice came through, "We got him, Cesar. Your man was hit."

Cesar and Paulo looked at each other, "That's not possible. It's not Miguel they got," yelled Cesar.

Paulo started the car and they took off on a dirt road east toward the mountain. They reached the end of the road and hurried on foot toward the place where the hit had happened. Paulo climbed the slope faster and got to the edge of the gully first.

"I can't see anybody here. There's only a mound of fresh dirt at the bottom. Wait, I see something. Madre de Dios! There's a hand sticking out. There's somebody buried here."

Cesar got there out of breath. Paulo was digging in the dirt around the hand with his police stick and flashlight. Cesar got into the gully and helped him. After a few minutes they could see a shoulder and they dug faster towards the neck and head. Paulo finally used his hands to clear the dirt and gravel around the face. At first they looked at the bloodied face without recognizing the buried man.

"It's Rodrigo! These asses killed Rodrigo!" Paulo shouted. He kept digging feverishly, and in a couple of minutes the torso was out. They grabbed Rodrigo under the arms and slowly pulled him out from his rocky grave. His left leg was broken and bent abnormally below the knee.

"You hold him Paulo, I'll free his leg."

They laid him a few feet from the mound of earthen debris. Paulo bent down and brushed the dirt from his chest. As he did so he heard a muffled rattling sound from Rodrigo's throat.

"Wait, I hear something!" He put his ear on his chest and heard a faint breathing now. "He is still alive!" He stuck his ear near the heart. "Yes, he is alive! We got to get help in a hurry!" Cesar took off running to the car parked about five hundred yards further down. He could hear the chatter of voices on the radio. He yelled into the microphone, "Send a helicopter! We have a wounded man."

"Is it an accident?" asked the voice on the receiving side.

"No! It's pure stupidity! He was shot by the drone. They got the wrong man. They got Rodrigo, Manuel's nephew! We need a helicopter over here immediately to take him to the hospital. Hurry!"

The helicopter with two men on board flew over the ridge of the Baboquivari Mountains, descended slowly and hovered over the police car, then flew back up to where the policemen were signaling to land. A paramedic jumped out, carrying a gurney, and ran toward the wounded form on the ground. He quickly examined Rodrigo to find where he was wounded, then tied him onto the gurney to immobilize him. Rodrigo was conscious now and kept moaning, asking for help. They latched him onto the helicopter and it took off over the ridge toward Tucson.

Paulo and Cesar drove back to the road where they had spied on Miguel. They looked all around with their binoculars. All they could see were mesquite branches waving gently in the wind. They walked to the place they'd last seen him. They saw fresh footprints in the wash their target had crossed, and further down a whole lot more of older footprints where everything became confused. They walked back to their car and drove away.

Miguel stayed under the canopy of the mesquite branches. He could not see where the drone had gone. He had heard a loud explosion and then silence. Then he heard a car drive off. He crawled to a point where he could see better and recognized a police car. They had been close to him and he had not even known it. Whatever the explosion was, it helped him. It made the police take off that way. When he could not hear the car anymore, he got up and resumed his escape to the south. Walking as fast as he could, he saw the Baboquivari Mountain range getting lower, and he knew he was approaching the border.

He stopped and took out his GPS. He was close to a place called Newfield. He slanted to the east for a place between Newfield and Buenos Aires. When he was a mile from the border he climbed a small mound and checked the surrounding area. There was no trace of human beings. He continued straight south now and took another GPS reading. His GPS indicated that he was in Mexico. A quarter mile straight ahead, there was a hill with a volcanic black rock on top. He climbed it and looked around searching for Dolores and her car.

There she was! Exactly where they had agreed two days ago. He waved, and she saw him, and she waved back. He hurried down the hill and twenty minutes later, he was in her arms. He hugged her with delight and she sobbed joyful tears. He was home.

Chapter 15

El Pato was waiting for the doctor's verdict with apprehension. The physician read charts and wrote comments on them. He finally looked at El Pato with a smile. "I have to say, you're lucky. You won't need surgery on your lower back. It will be painful for a few days, and you're going to have to take it easy, but physical therapy should be enough. You'll stay here today, and we'll make a decision tomorrow about when to release you. As for your tibia, it's set correctly and time is what you need to heal it. I'm going to have you come back—we'll tell you more when we release you—so we can look at it again. But for now you're as good as you can possibly be."

"Can I walk around? I hate staying in bed."

"I don't see why not. Take it easy, and use your crutches. Check with the nurses, they are in charge of that. I'll see you again tomorrow."

El Pato finished his breakfast, interrupted by the doctor's visit, and hopped out of his room. He hobbled across the hallway to a large window looking out on the street. The sun was rising, and the traffic was picking up. The hospital had good food and excellent care. Still, he wished he could leave right away. Hospital was better than jail, but not by much. He had a lot to do. He had botched his plans. He was not able to interrogate Miguel or Rodrigo, and by the time he got out, they would have gone into hiding. How was he to get his merchandise back?

So far he had been lucky, as the doctor said. Not just on the physical aspect, but also with the police. With no previous record, they did not suspect anything. All they had on him was a ticket for careless driving. He'd been able to give the law a song and dance to explain how he ended up in the gully. Lucky also that Mario had managed to make himself scarce before anybody found him. Officially, he had been alone in the truck and a moment of distraction had caused the accident.

On the darker side, he had a lot to fear. This was the first new type of shipment he was supposed to handle, and it was a complete failure. The value of this shipment, cocaine mixed with pot, was more than ten times that of previous deliveries. Cesar was to be taken out of the loop, and a new boss would contact him. He was to show his ability to handle this shipment before they trusted him with bigger jobs. Instead, disaster had struck. Rodrigo had introduced a grain of sand in the gears of the mechanism and it came to a halt. He was sure Miguel was the cause. He had tried to kidnap Miguel and Rodrigo, and Manuel with them, recover the shipment, and get the gears turning again. Now he would have to run. They would blame him. The monster without a face would be out to kill him. He didn't know who his new boss was. His last hope had been to get back the shipment. Now his very survival was in question.

He turned around to hop back to his room. As he passed by the nurses' station, a priest came out of a room two doors down from his own. The priest looked at him. El Pato quickly looked away. Priests are bad luck. They show up when death is around, like vultures. He wondered who had died in that room. He got back to the nurses' station after the priest had gone and asked one of them, "Who died in that room?"

"Which room?"

"I saw a priest come out from that room over there."

"Nobody died. The priest came because the patient in that room asked for him."

"Why? Is he going to die? What happened to him?"

"You're a funny one! He could have died. He was brought in by helicopter, but he did not die, and he is improving fast."

"A helicopter? It must have been a serious accident. What happened?"

"They flew him in from the Tohono O'odham lands. I heard he was shot by Border Patrol. Mistaken identity, they say. That's near where you were picked up, isn't it?"

"Yes. So he's not going to die? I might know him. I know some people there. Can I talk to him?"

"You can, if he wants to. He's eating breakfast now. Give him time. Keep it short. He's still in pain."

El Pato looked into the room, hesitatingly. A young man was sitting up on his bed, pale, with an IV in his left arm, his right leg immobilized in a large cast. A bowl of fruit and a glass of orange juice were on a tray by the bedside. He looked at El Pato with a questioning smile, and El Pato spoke.

"Hola! I just came to take a look at the surviving hero shot at by La Migra. How are you feeling, hombre? My name is Xavier Diaz. Call me El Pato."

"Hi, El Pato! Rodrigo Cruz. I have felt better, but I'm glad to be alive."

El Pato was stunned. This was Manuel's nephew! He had to be careful. "You were shot in the leg?"

"No. A drone fired at me. I fell in a ditch and they missed me, but not by much."

"Where did this happen? Why would they do that? Since

when are they using drones?"

"They told me I was the first ever. They apologized. They said it was all a big mistake. They took me for somebody else. It happened near San Miguel, on Tohono O'odham land."

"I can't believe it! I don't know what to say. On your own lands? And how did it happen?"

"I was following a friend who was returning home to Mexico. I was a half mile behind him, above the bajada. He was walking further down. It's him they were after. Why? I don't know. Miguel's never done anything wrong."

El Pato paled. He was with Miguel, the man he had tried to kidnap. Maybe all was not lost. A sudden hope rose in him that somehow he could escape his fate. Rodrigo must have been in the truck with Miguel when he'd failed to stop them. He'd just seen a glimpse of three men in a white pickup as his truck made the one-eighty before leaving the road for the gully. Obviously Rodrigo had never heard of him, and that was good. Still, he had to be very careful. If Rodrigo asked him how he was injured, he would have to come up with a lie. He had to keep the conversation focused on Rodrigo and not himself.

"You're a lucky man, Rodrigo. Maybe not so lucky—you were at the wrong place at the wrong time—but you're very lucky to survive."

"Oh, it's nothing to do with luck. It's a good thing after all."

"A good thing? To be almost killed?"

"No, not that. Do me a favor, El Pato, lower my bed, I want to lie down. My back's sore sitting up."

El Pato reached for the remote control and lowered the head of the bed to a more horizontal position. "Better?"

"Yeah, thanks."

"What about that good thing?"

"It's what happened after that is good."

"What happened?"

"They missed me. I fell in a deep gully. A lot of dirt and gravel fell on me. I passed out. When I came to, I was in complete darkness. I thought I was dead and buried. I couldn't do nothing. I was scared, unable to move." Rodrigo fell silent for a moment, remembering.

He was buried in a tomb of rocks and dirt in the bottom of the gully. Why had he been targeted? It must have been a mistake, he thought. It seemed like the end of everything. A victory scored for randomness. One minute he was walking, watching his friend Miguel, and the next, unaccountably, he was buried alive. There was hope and good intentions, and then nothingness—no further goal ahead. Was nothingness the future imposed on him?

He rebelled against it. He refused it and looked with all his will toward a goal beyond this fateful event. In desolation, he forced himself to advance toward a different future. Unable to move any part of his body, he concentrated on opposing the compulsion to surrender to meaninglessness. Fighting panic, he waited for some unseen good to come forth.

He was pleased to find that it was possible to fight the onslaught of despair. In his hope for goodness, there was first a space where he could think and hope, a potential for willing freely. He chose to stay in that oasis of freedom. He trusted that there was a purpose for him in his situation. Was there a celestial favor in this? Manuel and others had talked about such things, but he had paid little attention. He could barely breathe and his whole body ached.

There was a further choice to make: accept the situation not because he hoped to stay alive and return to his former life, but because he was willing to give up his previous life in exchange for a completely different one. It was a choice between mortality and immortality. Death was abhorrent to him. Would he let go and step out with courage into the blinding light of the incomprehensible? He asked the light to come to him.

A faint dawn reached through the rocks and dirt. He felt a hand touch his hand. He was extricated from the tomb.

"El Pato, have you ever done things you're ashamed of?"

El Pato averted his eyes, looking for the right words. He was ashamed of his failure to handle his first big assignment correctly; ashamed of his acts in a moral sense, he never thought of that. He wanted to find out more about Rodrigo's dealings with Miguel. Maybe the young man was still in shock from the accident and would talk.

"Rodrigo, there are a lot of things I have done that I am ashamed of."

"I'm alive because I accepted to give up my past. Everything I did before was defeated. I was buried alive and my pride was removed like hair from my head—like being scalped. Yes, I was scalped, and my scalp was stuck on a lance and presented to me. I had to take it and renounce it. It was the price of passing into a new life."

El Pato looked at the young man, his face pale against the white pillows, but his eyes shining with a strange inner light. He had been one of the 'worker ants', as Cesar liked to describe his unknowing employees. He carried merchandise from Sureño to Del Norte. Rodrigo did not know whom he worked for. He had been trained to ask no questions, to simply recognize the load he was to pick up, carry it to another place, and dump it there. He had done it for months, for a few dollars. Now he was changed. El Pato couldn't help admiring him. He had been freed from slavery. He was looking at a free man.

He, on the other hand, was still caught in a trap. No

admission of error would mollify his new boss. He was bound to death. Who could free him?

"Who found you and dug you out?"

"I have no clue."

Rodrigo seemed genuine, even though a bit strange. Maybe it was easier for him to escape the trap—he was only a worker ant. Was there a way out for El Pato too?

"What was the priest doing here with you?"

"I confessed to him."

"You believe in that?"

"To be freed from your past, you must renounce meaninglessness and choose to see good come out of bad. That was the condition of my freedom. Once you are scalped, like I was, you tell the truth, no matter what."

"To be so truthful, as you say, that can be dangerous."

"Why dangerous?"

"You never know who you are talking to. If you reveal too much, it might cost you your life."

"That's why you need confession. Then you can look at the other guy as a brother. You welcome him."

El Pato thought about it for a few seconds. "Rodrigo, do you know who I am?"

"Xavier Diaz, or El Pato, that's what you said."

"No, I mean, who I really am, inside."

"You want to confess to me? You need a priest."

"Let me tell you. I'm the guy who sent you a message to tell you bad things would happen if you didn't deliver the merchandise to me, at the place I would decide."

"Small world, El Pato! Now we are both banged up. How did you get injured?"

El Pato hesitated, but continued, "I'm the one who tried to

stop you on your way home to ask serious questions of your friend Miguel and you."

"I didn't recognize you. You're not the man with the pistol."

"I didn't recognize you either."

"Why say this now?"

"To see if you are truthful. What happened to the merchandise?"

"It's gone for good. It's at the bottom of a deep cave. Impossible to get to it. Nobody can get down there."

"And what was Miguel doing in this?"

"He was going to Colorado somewhere, and injured his knee carrying a dying woman on his back. We took him in to let him rest. He is now gone back to his family in Mexico."

"Why did you go to Tucson and meet with a bunch of other people there?"

"To meet Miguel's wife. She was worried about him not being able to come back as he had planned."

"Why didn't you deliver the merchandise as planned?"

"I was told by Sureño that the police were after me. I took it to Manuel's place. Then Miguel showed up. He saw the merchandise and recognized it was cocaine, not pot. So we all decided this was too hot for us, and dumped it in the pit in the cave."

El Pato remained silent for a long time, thinking. He was amazed. The worker ant had answered all his questions as if they were simple everyday questions. He expected him to be scared, to hide, to cover things up. He was really truthful, as he said. This whole thing was just a big screw up, nothing but bad luck.

"Tell me, El Pato, why do you think you and me are here, both banged up but alive?"

"Luck, good or bad, who knows?"

"You don't see anything in it? You try to find me for days, you try to stop us on the highway to force us to talk, you get banged up, and the next day it's my turn. We're brought to the same hospital, next to each other, and you don't see anything in it at all?"

"I'm no visionary. Nobody gave me a new life."

"I'm sure you're here because I'm supposed to pass on to you what I received. It's the same question for you. Choose—life or death. It's your turn. Go for it!"

El Pato felt defeated. Usually he was careful to maintain his superiority, to remain in control. A strange thing was happening. He felt that, to escape from the death trap, it was necessary to make the same choice Rodrigo had made. Renouncing his former life was going to be painful—a real scalping for sure. Without the merchandise he could make no amends to his new boss. Lost forever as it was, according to Rodrigo, this was a real bad situation. There was no going back, no way to avoid punishment. Could any good really come out from a seriously flawed past?

A nurse came in to take the breakfast plates away. Another came to take Rodrigo's blood pressure. El Pato left in silence and made his way back to his room.

The room was in darkness, as he had left it after the doctor's visit. A ray of sunshine extended from the east window across the hallway to the edge of the door. He hopped to the window and lifted the shade. The light came in.

He reached for the crutches and walked out into the hallway. The same nurse he had seen after the doctor left came toward him. He stopped her. "Where is that priest that came out from Rodrigo's room?"

"Why? Do you think you are dying?" she teased him.

"I feel I have to do some dying so I can live again. Can you call him back to talk to me?"

"Are you serious?"

"Absolutely... excuse me, nurse, I never asked your name. What is it?"

"Anastasia."

"That's beautiful. What does it mean?"

"Resurrection."

"Ah, yes! That's what I need—resurrection!"

Manuel, Roger, and Hank tiptoed into the room, hesitatingly. Rodrigo seemed to be asleep. They had turned around to leave when he opened his eyes and called them back. They asked him to tell the story of his miraculous survival. He did so obligingly. Then he added, "Guess who's on the same floor, two rooms down from here... El Pato."

"Who is he?" asked Manuel.

"The man who attempted to run us off the highway. And guess who else he is."

"You better tell us."

"He's the one who sent me that threatening note about the merchandise."

"Does he know who you are?" asked Manuel.

"Yes, I had a good talk with him this morning. He thought Miguel was trying to steal his merchandise. He was attempting to kidnap us to question us."

"And the police—do they know about him?"

"No."

"Should we tell them?"

"No. El Pato's ready for some new things in his life. I talked to him, and he said he wanted to experience the same change I did when I was buried under the dirt. I believe he's not kidding. He's really changing inside."

"I'll have a word with this character. Where is he?"

"Two doors further down."

Manuel stormed out toward El Pato's door. Thirty seconds later he was back, looking puzzled. "Can't believe this. I saw it with my own eyes. His door was almost shut. I peered through, and you won't believe this, your neighbor has a priest in there with him. The priest is wearing his stole. El Pato is confessing or something."

"So he followed the advice," smiled Rodrigo.

"You gave him advice?"

"He saw the priest who came to hear my confession and asked me about it. I told him he needed the same thing."

Manuel stood in amazement. "You, Rodrigo, talked to a priest and you confessed? That's a first! How did you get through to this El Pato?"

"I don't know. I told him what happened to me."

"And what happened to you?"

"I told him to expect to see the good come out of bad events like mine, for example."

Manuel and Roger looked at each other with disbelief.

"You now believe in celestial favors?"

"My pride was removed from my head. I told El Pato it was like being scalped. He understood."

"How can you change so fast?" asked Hank. Rodrigo shrugged his shoulders. He didn't know.

"Once you surrender, things can change fast," suggested Roger. "It's our glacial pace of surrendering that holds things up."

Manuel regained his wits after a moment. "Sobrino, I don't know why it happened, but whatever happened was worth it. I can hardly recognize you. So what do you think we should do?"

"Leave El Pato alone. Miguel had a target on his back. They tried to kill him. I was almost killed. El Pato could have been killed. All these plans were disasters. It's time to change. El Pato's now a friend. Tell me, did Miguel get home safely?"

"Yes. Dolores called Francesca this morning," explained Roger. "We will call them back to tell them the good news about your recovery and your sudden change. They'll be surprised."

"It was all that rehearsing with your choir. You all got me ready for this."

Chapter 16

Every time Hank looked at his wife, Kim, he was reminded of what he had lost. She had become even more attractive since she left him—slim, athletic, with a somewhat shorter hairdo. A red coral necklace smartly highlighted her reddish hair and contrasted with her turquoise floral print dress with a gold belt that emphasized her svelteness. Cobalt blue and gold earrings sculpted as small eagle feathers dangled against her slender neck. He recognized them as the pair he had given her a few months before she left him. A few wrinkles around her mouth betrayed her otherwise youthful allure. She was pleasant and polite, but remained at a distance, like an Apache trout caught once before and now wary of any lure.

Celine ran toward them and grabbed Hank's hand. "Come see, Daddy, Mommy, there's a big black snake around the corner." They followed her as she ran back toward the little man-made brook in the center of the Tohono Chul Park. She looked around, searching for the snake.

"There it is! See it?"

Hank and Kim caught sight of a dark tail slithering into a dense bush, where it disappeared.

"What kind of a snake was it, daddy?"

"I didn't see much of it, but it could have been a black king snake.”

“Are they dangerous?”

“Not if you leave them alone, sweetheart.”

Celine ran towards the desert turtles’ enclosure.

“What time is your flight tomorrow?” asked Hank.

“Oh, one o’clock, I believe.”

“That doesn’t give us much time to talk. It’s already three o’clock.”

“We don’t need much time. We had years to talk, and it didn’t help.”

“You don’t believe in reconciliation?”

“I didn’t say that, but it’s not probable.”

“Your mind is made up? You want a divorce?”

“What else is there? It’s been long enough—two years almost. Why wait longer?”

“When you’re not sure, you’re supposed to wait and not rush. Wait for a sign.”

“A sign? From whom?”

“Maybe... a celestial favor.”

“I don’t know what that is. I tried everything, Hank—seducing you, wooing you. Nothing worked. You were the unconquerable, unapproachable hero. I failed. I’m tired of it. I don’t want to try again.”

“We failed because we didn’t do it right. We didn’t act as a couple. We followed our individual desires. We went our separate paths like two comets. One around the sun and shining, the other an invisible mass of ice lost in faraway darkness.”

“I felt like the moon—dead and cold.”

She had not forgotten the bits of astronomy they used to discuss in happier days. Hank reached for her hand. Kim stepped away to examine a fairy duster bush.

"We don't look in the same direction any more, Kim. We don't sing together, or even just talk."

Kim did not look back. "We never sang together. Did you join a choir recently?"

"Yes, I found a choir. We don't really sing; we support each other. It's a great help. When one falters the others pull him up. You could join the choir too."

"Who are they?"

"One is an engineer. One is a young man who used to traffic in drugs. Another is his uncle—an old friend of mine—who hid the drugs and got rid of them. Another is a foreigner who came in illegally and got back to his country recently. They are gifts of Providence."

"Some gifts they are! And you keep company with such people? You're not afraid they will get you in trouble with the law?"

"No. They help me view reality differently, adapt to daily demands. I learned how to expect good things to come out of bad ones."

"I would stay away from them if I were you," she said, turning toward him with a look of real concern on her face.

"What is more important than discovering goodness, truth, and beauty, as they come out of all things, as a favor to us?" As he said this, Hank was taking in the quiet loveliness all around. His daughter was part of it; he was part of it; so was Kim, even if she didn't realize it.

Kim looked away and said slowly, "I have never seen good come out of evil. I have tried to keep myself and Celine as far away from evil as possible."

"Can you tell what's good and what's evil? Do you know what truth is?"

"Stop, Hank! I try my best. It's not easy."

"That's why we need a choir. When it sings the song of Providence, the choir shows us the meaning of what it is to be human, the meaning of love and how to reach it. We need that."

"Maybe it works for you, Hank. I rely on my own truth. And besides, the members of your choir don't inspire confidence."

"So you're giving up on us? What about Celine?"

Kim folded her arms and took two steps away. "The court will determine when you can see her and how long. When she grows up, she can make up her own mind."

In the parking lot, Celine clung to her daddy for a long time, then she turned away and ran to Kim's car to hide her tears.

The next morning after breakfast Kim was packing the suitcases. She was wearing her travel clothes: jeans, jean jacket, and comfortable loafers. Celine had matching jeans and a cute polo shirt decorated with three young owls perched on a branch.

"Did you pack your toothbrush?" asked Kim.

"Yes, mommy, I'm all packed."

The telephone rang. The front desk was asking her to come to the lobby. There was a Border Patrol agent who wanted to talk to her. Kim was surprised. She didn't know why Border Patrol would want to talk to her. The receptionist gave the phone to the agent. He said he would explain everything—it was only a formality. He assured her it was not a big deal. Celine insisted she wanted to come too, so both went down to the lobby.

The lobby was decorated with a large Christmas tree twinkling with multicolored lights and two reindeer pulling a small sleigh filled with beautifully wrapped gifts. The receptionist pointed out the agent, who was seated behind the reindeer, reading a newspaper. Kim and Celine walked over to him.

The agent introduced himself as Mario. He wore a uniform with a badge and apologized for the inconvenience. He explained it had to do with her husband, Hank. They wanted her to answer a few questions about some people Hank had been associated with lately. She said she didn't know about Hank's whereabouts for the past year. She had only come to town to resolve a personal matter.

She told herself her premonition had been right, the day before, while talking to Hank. He should have steered clear of that group—what did he call them, a choir? The faster she left town the better. Mario reassured her there was no question about Hank himself, only some people he knew and their relationship with somebody else they might have known. It would greatly help if she could verify some activities of her husband in the past. Only a few questions, that's all. The whole matter would take half an hour at most. They would just ask her and Hank a few questions and that would be the end of it. They would pick Hank up at his office at the University; afterwards he would bring them back immediately. He had a car waiting outside. Kim looked at her watch. They had plenty of time before departing to the airport. If this took about an hour, they would be back in time to check out. She sighed. "OK but we've got to be back in an hour, So let's go and be quick." Celine was excited; she wanted to see her daddy again.

As Mario was driving west on Speedway, his phone rang and he listened silently for a few seconds. He looked at Kim and Celine in the back seat.

"That was my boss. He's just a few blocks away. He wants to take you personally to your interview. That's good. He can make things happen faster. You'll be back in no time."

As they approached the University, Mario steered into a parking lot where there was a white van with Border Patrol markings. Mario parked, opened the doors for his passengers, and helped them out. A man in his mid-fifties, dressed in a western outfit with hat and boots, came out of the van and walked over.

"Thank you for coming, Ma'am. My name is Tito. I'll take care of you now. Mario, you go get Professor Wagner and then we'll all go together to that meeting. It won't take long." He turned toward Kim and Celine. "Why don't you sit in the van and make yourselves comfortable. I have bottles of water if you want."

Kim said she wasn't thirsty; neither was Celine. They followed the Border Patrol officer to the van.

"I appologize for the bench seats," continued Tito. "I use this van sometimes to deport illegals to Mexico. That's why there's the grille that separates the front seats from the back of the van. Good thing we're not going far. You won't have time to get uncomfortable."

Kim shrugged her shoulders. "It's OK with me. It can't be any worse than air travel is these days."

Mario found a space to park in the visitors' lot and entered the astronomy department building. He found Hank's office and knocked. The door was half open, but there was nobody inside. As he hesitated, Hank came down the hallway and asked if he was looking for him. Mario said he worked for Border Patrol and would be grateful if Hank came with him to answer a few questions about Manuel and Rodrigo's guest, Miguel. Hank answered that he knew Miguel had been a guest at Manuel's house, but he had departed by now. Mario knew that. It was just a formality to clear Manuel and his nephew. They only needed some general information from him. "We have your wife with us," the agent explained. "She'll have to sign a deposition."

"Kim is here too?" wondered Hank.

"Yes, and Celine with her. She insisted she wanted to see you again. They're in my boss's car around the corner. I'll drive you there."

Hank grabbed his jacket and followed Mario. When they got to the van, Hank was clearly delighted to see his wife again. Celine hugged him and sat next to him. Mario took the wheel, with Tito in the passenger seat, and they took off.

Along the way, the affable Tito was explaining where they were going. It was right next to the airport. They took Campbell and Kino Parkway south. Tito's phone rang. He listened for a minute and turned to his passengers.

"There's a change in plans. They want to show some evidence and want you to come to the site of the incident. It's a bit farther west on Ajo Way. I'm sorry for this slight delay."

"If I miss my plane, you'll have to pay our extra fare, you know," Kim cut back, irritated.

"No problem, lady," answered Tito, "trust me, you'll not miss your plane."

Hank was becoming suspicious. He glanced at Kim. She only seemed concerned about making the plane. Celine looked at her daddy with questioning eyes. He looked at her owl-decorated shirt. "What does it say? 'Whooo looks out for yooo?' I do, that's whoo!"

Celine squeezed against her daddy, somewhat reassured.

Hank did not like the turn of events. There was no evidence to show. Furthermore, Ajo Way became Ajo Highway and went through the Tohono O'odham lands. There was no Border Patrol office there, only roadblocks sometimes. He checked the van's doors. They were locked and could be unlocked only by the driver. This did not look to him to be on the level. He thought about what to do.

"Just where are we going, and why?" his wife questioned.

Hank lifted up his hands and slapped his thighs. "Can't fight City Hall, as they say. We'll see soon, I hope."

Kim turned away her face in disgust.

He had to stay calm. If he challenged Tito, Kim and Celine could panic. There was nothing he could do. They could not escape, even if they stopped at some intersection. He breathed deeply to relax. Would something good come out of this? If you don't know what to do, wait for a celestial favor. He put his arm around Celine and pressed her against his side.

The van was now approaching the Tohono O'odham lands. Leaning against the window, Hank could see some of the domes of the observatory on top of Kitt Peak. This was the route he took to go to his favorite work, when he got away from all the attachments and concentrated on the pure world of abstraction and science. He used to see his work as a conquest of the world, a sort of prize he bestowed on Kim and Celine. He had the pleasure of giving it but he would have disdained to be thanked for it. He preferred to be King Midas, respected from afar. It was his duty and privilege; that was enough.

He saw the hills drawing together, the road dipping into washes that flooded with torrents of rainwater in the monsoon season. How many times had he looked at them as an inconvenience and obstacles delaying his arrival at his kingly throne? Now he wished to stop and walk down each gully, admire the force of the passing water that carved deep furrows in the rocks, like arteries conducting the blood of the world toward mysterious organs underground that gave life to the mountains, the bajada, and the desert below. The inanimate objects looked back at him lovingly, calling him to slow down and enjoy their restful peace. They cared about him and Kim and Celine, while the van driver and Tito seemed to be material objects. The hills and ravines were his body, speaking to him about his love for his work, his love for his wife and daughter. They had witnessed his unspoken devotion to them for years. They had known his true feelings, buried deep under the rock. He had been a silent object unable to sing, while they had softly chanted the praise of his patience, his strength, and his love each time he had driven by. Who had given them this ability to know him better than he knew himself? There was a presence in them that shouted to be recognized. Was it too late? He began to see reality as it truly was: nature, man and Providence linked together as one. Everything could be reborn and transformed.

He glanced again at his wife. He saw a wounded dove with broken wings, unable to fly, awaiting her fate. He could not tell her all this. She had turned away from him. But when man cannot speak, nature will speak for him. Could the hills and mountains speak to her for him? He wished he could take that wounded bird, his precious dove, inside him to shield her from all this. Was his love for her powerful enough to protect her? All he had now was this love. All else was absent, except the hills and gullies outside, and what they stood for. They stood for his feeble love, but behind it, vaguely perceptible to him for the first time, was the power that created the mountains and the hills and the oceans, and brought the moon close to the earth to make it livable. That power condensed dark globules and ignited the fire of fusion inside stars. That loving power had created him, his wounded dove, and Celine. The celestial gift was there. It would have to take over.

It had come too soon, only three days after El Pato's release from the hospital. He knew it had to come, but he had hoped for time to enjoy the Christmas season, for a few more days of gaining strength and confidence in his new life. But Mario came to pick him up two days before Christmas. If only Christmas could have come before this was settled, he would have been delighted. But Mario had come first, and El Pato felt dejected. Mario was now going to take him to meet their new boss, and he was excited, saying, "You'll never guess who he is, El Pato."

No, he would have never guessed. The mysterious lord of the cocaine traffic, the one taking over from Cesar, was Tito, who worked for La Migra. Mario was bubbling with enthusiasm. "Can you imagine? This is going to be easy for us! Tito knows what La Migra is doing from the inside, and he can plan his shipments and deliveries so that everything moves smoothly, undisturbed. We'll just have to deal with Cesar and his sidekick Paulo and switch over to the new organization."

Mario was taking him to meet Tito so he could give them his orders for future shipments. He painted a future of ease and near bliss, with reduced risks and money stuffed in their pockets. El Pato let him talk, but he didn't see it that way. There was the question of the missing shipment. Mario avoided all reference to that detail. Maybe Mario knew more than he wanted to reveal. There was something forced in his attitude of pleasantness. When asked where they were going, El Pato detected nervousness in his response. "To La Cienega Del Coyote. Tito wants a private place for our first meeting. You know where it is, don't you?"

Yes, El Pato knew. They were retracing the same route they had taken on that fateful day when they had attempted, unsuccessfully, to kidnap Miguel and Rodrigo, and Manuel had dodged the trap. Then, he had been in charge. He'd given orders to Mario, and he'd laid a trap for others. Now Mario was driving him to an uncertain destiny and he was riding, with a bad back and broken leg, into a trap others had laid for him, dumb and unknowing, like a lamb taken to be slaughtered. They passed the place where the accident had happened. "We almost exited from life, right here," snickered Mario, shaking his head. "We were lucky, both of us. Don't you think?" El Pato remained silent.

He was so far from that day that it seemed another time, lost in the mist of a distant past. The world that he had constructed for himself had collapsed in ruins, burying him underneath, like Rodrigo. A new life had started the moment he had taken the young man's advice to surrender and be seized. Until then, God, for him, had meant death. Any encounter with religious people, mostly priests, had an odor of death, and he instinctively avoided them. Now he knew why. It was the death of his own will that he'd wanted to avoid, all that time. It took the complete collapse of his plans, his utter failure to perform in his first big cocaine shipment, to force him to come to grips with this will stronger than his own. This was the will he had recoiled from, even in his youth. When his own will was impotent, he was dumbfounded that this other will was coming to his rescue, with the intent of freeing him.

His meeting with the priest in the hospital had been a first step. He'd accused himself of running away from this will. He'd declared what he had considered the summit of his accomplishments—his emergence into a position of dominance where he made life and death decisions for others—to be errors. The priest asked him to clarify, did he consider all that to be sins, and he'd admitted they were sins. Then the priest used the name of that unknown will that had the power to forgive sins and bring the dead to life because it had conquered sin and death, and cleansed his past. He felt hands remove an enormous weight from his shoulders, hands like that of a warrior, hands used to wielding heavy weapons, and his feet became warm, as if somebody had washed and wiped them. Those mighty hands had a gentle touch.

He took that memory home with him when he was released

from the hospital. He, Xavier Diaz, who flew at the sight of priests like a duck from hunters, had started to address this unknown will. And, amazingly, he could not only address it, it responded. Maybe that's what his mother used to call prayer. Over the next two days he'd had wordless conversations with the will that was becoming less unknown. It was not a sweet encounter, it was very much *mano a mano*. The will was asserting itself in him. It asked for things in return. The most disconcerting thing was that he had to give up all his plans, even his plans about how to follow that will. He had, until now, gone where he wanted to go, and done what he pleased, but the time was now coming when he would be taken, against his will, to places he did not want to go. And he should not hesitate, because the presence of the will was always going to be ahead of him, and he should not try to understand, just accept to be led. That had bothered him at first. He'd rationalized that there were things for him to do. He would prepare himself during Christmas, the birth of the new life that dispels the darkness. Then he would be ready for whatever came.

When Mario called, he knew it was the trip to the place he did not want to go. There was sadness in him. He would have liked more time to taste what life could be, working in the open, without threats and without having to hide. At the same time, there was an amazing joy budding in him. He knew the victory would be his if he did the right thing. It was the nature of what he had to do that surprised him. His whole life had been a vigorous flight from any encounter with death. His failures had been openings through which death could rush in to get hold of him and drown him in an eternity of dark nothingness. He had fought with all his might to plug any such hole before it could destroy his plans. Now that all his strength had gone, with a broken leg and a painful back, he was going to meet his failures and there was no escaping them using any of his old skills.

What he had been trying to avoid was now coming to meet him. Now he could see, like a dust storm roaring through the desert, a column of warriors, all experts at war, with swords drawn to chase away his fear of the coming battle. And then the warriors surrounded him and their leader approached him, holding a lance. There was a scalp hanging from it. The leader asked him to take it. It was the scalp of an enemy that had been defeated. All he had to do was to take it. He hesitated.

A battle raged inside him, voices shouting to give up this madness that could not be true. He fought vigorously to cut down the lies surrounding him, the lies he had taken for truths and accepted as friends and that now attacked him on all sides, trying to separate him from the company of the warriors. He tried to break through toward the warrior still holding the scalp on the spear. As he made his move, he felt a sting on the left side of his chest. He thought he was going to die, but the warrior pushed through to him and pulled him to his side, in the middle of the circle of his warriors, and gave him the scalp of the dead enemy on the spear. Xavier shuddered when he took the scalp. It was his own. His pride had been killed. He stood in the midst of the group. He was now one of them.

"That's where we turn," Xavier heard Mario say. They were just beyond the place where the accident happened. They turned south on a narrow road and after a short while turned west on a primitive trail. "This is where Tito is waiting."

It used to be a gathering place for cattle about to be taken to the market, in the days when the Tohono O'odham raised cattle. Now it was a place nobody visited.

After a few miles of a bumpy ride, they drove up to a van parked in front of a collapsed gate; beyond it, a narrow passage into a box canyon opened into what used to be a corral. The natural enclosure, a circular area of about four acres, was formed by the foothills of the Quinlan Mountains. Right in the center there was a shrine to La Guadalupe, in the form of a half circle of old adobe bricks. In its middle, painted white, was a small statue of the Virgin.

At first they didn't see anybody. Right against a wall of rocks that climbed toward the summit of Kitt Peak, where a few observatory domes could be seen, there was a clump of mesquite trees. Tito emerged from the trees, dressed as a cattle rancher: cowboy boots, belt buckle embedded with turquoise stones, a black leather coat, dark red shirt, and a wide brimmed hat. He walked toward them, arms extended in a friendly greeting.

"Bienvenido, El Pato, I'm Tito, your boss from now on. I'm glad you could come. We have a lot to talk about."

"Hola, Tito. I couldn't refuse the ride. Call me Xavier," said El Pato, as they shook hands.

"Why the new name?" Tito was puzzled.

"I have stopped flying away from danger like a duck."

Tito brushed his mustache, amused. "Mario must have told you the news. I'm taking over the whole organization. Cesar is out. I'm the one you report to from now on."

"Yes, Mario told me. Why the change?"

"You should know, Xavier. Things didn't go as planned. You didn't receive the shipment and you didn't deliver it. That's not acceptable. Two hundred kilos of drugs cannot disappear from the surface of the earth without leaving a trace. We must correct that."

"I can't deliver what I don't have."

"True, El Pato—sorry, Xavier, if you wish. But we're here to make things right. Cesar is now out. His involvement with the tribal police is no help anymore. We need better connections, and I have them. But our suppliers in Vera Cruz will not stand for unaccounted merchandise. We must get it back. I heard you have tried to recover it already, but without success. That's good, but not good enough. I'm here to help you succeed. Here's what I want you to do. You know the merchandise is somewhere in the hands of Manuel. His nephew is still in the hospital. He's just a pawn. We need Manuel to reveal the exact location where our shipment is stashed away. You tell him we have his friends here and we'll punish them if he doesn't show up."

"What friends?"

Tito took a few steps toward the clump of mesquite trees and called for Hank to come forward. At the same time, he pulled a gun from his coat pocket and pointed it at the newcomers. Hank came first, followed by Celine and a disconsolate Kim.

"You know them, El Pato, don't you?"

He remembered vaguely the man. He'd caught a glimpse of him when he tagged Manuel's pickup at Roger's place in Tucson. The woman and the girl he had never seen.

"Why are they here?" he asked.

"Hank is a dear friend of Manuel. I decided to add his wife and daughter to make it more convincing. If Manuel cares about them, he'll come. If not, you'll tell him his friends will be killed."

"Why me? Call him yourself."

"No, I won't. He must not know I exist until he gets here. I'll take care of him when he's here. You do the invitations. That's why we brought you here, to show what you got Manuel's friends into. You have no choice. You'll help us now. I want you to invite him here and we'll make him talk, and we'll get back the shipment. Can you do that?"

"It's not possible to get it back, Tito. I talked to Rodrigo in the hospital and he told me the merchandise had been thrown into a deep crevice in a cave. Nobody can get it back. It's lost."

"If that's true, it's bad news for all of you. We cannot leave any traces, even in a cave. I hope for your sake that he lied to you. Shipments must be accounted for or the responsible parties destroyed. No exception."

"You want me to bring Manuel here so you can dispose of everybody?"

"Don't be in a hurry. We first get the truth out of him. Maybe they lied. That would be good. Then we just find out where the shipment is, and we'll figure out what to do. I need you to get Manuel here to me."

"You want to kill him."

"What's that to you? That would be a lesson for you. You need to know how the new organization works. And we'll take care of Rodrigo later."

Xavier felt the battle was on. There was a threat in Tito's voice. If he cooperated, the blood of these innocents would be poured over his head. Who was he working for? It was time to decide.

"Frankly, Tito, I don't want to know how the organization works. I'm not in the organization anymore."

Tito's face became noticeably redder and his eyes showed contempt. "Oh, so El Pato, the duck, has flown the coop and hunts for himself now. Maybe you came here to receive your severance pay. Should I include any vacation time? You just walk out of here and I'll make a direct deposit to your account, is that it? Who do you think you work for?" Tito pointed the gun at him. "This is the only direct deposit you'll get from me, El Pato, or should I call you El Conejo? That's what you are, a trapped rabbit. Once you enter the organization there is no way out, except by abandoning your life."

"I know that, Tito. But I don't work for you."

"Who do you work for?" shouted Tito. "For Miguel, who deserted you, and ran back to Mexico? I'm not through with him yet. All I have to do is give his name to the organization and he's a dead man."

"That's the difference between your organization and mine, Tito. In your organization, you have to abandon your life if you want to quit. In the one I belong to, you have to abandon it in order to join."

"So you're a dead man?"

"I'm alive, but now my boss lives in me."

"You're crazy, hombre. Maybe it's better for you if I shoot you dead."

"I'm not crazy, Tito. You think of life as leading to death. I think of death as the gate to life. My boss asks me to surrender my life to him. I'll win if I accept to lose my life so he can give me his."

"Enough nonsense! Back to reality. Do what I told you!"

"Yes, let's get back to reality. You live in a phony world, Tito, a world of make-believe and lies. You say lies are good, and truth is bad. Wake up and free yourself. I'm here to pull you towards life and truth."

"You're here for only one reason—to answer my questions. Right now, truth is what I say. Truth is what I hold in my hand. It can destroy your truth in an instant. For the last time, will you obey me?"

"Understand one thing, Tito. I know now that my life was a preparation for this battle. I'm glad to accept this bargain. My death for the life of others, for the sake of the life I want."

"Who needs your senseless death?"

"You do, Tito. You'll need it from now on."

Tito raised his arm and shot Xavier, point blank in the face.

Kim screamed and grabbed Hank's arm. Hank put one arm around his wounded dove, and lifted Celine up in his other arm. Xavier collapsed and rolled on his side on the ground, moaning. Tito aimed at his chest on the left side and fired another shot. Xavier extended his right hand, reached for the spear with his scalp on it, grabbed it, and his lips pursed in the beginning of a smile. Then he lay motionless.

"You killed him!" Mario exclaimed. "What are we going to do now? Who is going to get Manuel to come here?"

"That's the difference between you and me, Mario. I know what to do. What we do next is bury this madman right behind the shrine of his new boss' mother."

They dragged the body fifty feet to a spot free of rocks and cacti. Tito sent Mario to the van, saying, "Take the key. I have a shovel and a pickaxe under the seats in the back."

"You always carry a shovel and a pickaxe with you, Tito?"

"You never know when you might need it, hombre."

Mario went to get the shovel and pickaxe, mumbling something inaudible. Tito made him dig a shallow grave, then they threw the body inside, with the crutches on top, and covered it with dirt and rocks.

Cesar had not heard from Tito since the day he'd botched up the attack on Miguel, allowing him to flee to Mexico and almost killing Rodrigo instead. Cesar had not been pleased with Tito's efficiency, but he avoided a confrontation with the man from ICE. Now Tito was proposing to meet and iron things out.

It was a convenient day for Cesar. He had the day off. Paulo was working by himself. He was surprised by the meeting place —a remote location on the east side of Kitt Peak, near the Coyote Wilderness. He had been there a couple of times in the past five years to check on reports of illegal immigrants using it as a staging spot where they would be picked up. In both cases it had been wrong information. The place was not visited by anybody anymore, but he remembered some kind of shrine was there, and somebody was still bringing flowers there once in a while —plastic flowers and some words written on folded pieces of paper, asking for the intercession of La Guadalupe.

Tito sounded to be in a conciliatory mood, but something raised Cesar's suspicion. There were plenty of other places, more convenient, where they could have met quietly. Why that one, so far from human eyes? Although Tito had not apologized for his poor handling of Miguel's escape, he sounded very friendly, maybe too friendly. Cesar decided to take some precautions. He called Paulo. They decided to meet immediately, on the west side of Baboquivari, at their old watching post where they could see Manuel's house high above.

"He wants me to meet him at noon, at La Cienega Del Coyote," Cesar explained.

"Must be important if he wants to see you. But why that place? That place gives me the creeps. It's full of ghosts of the past, things that didn't work out. Careful, Cesar," Paulo warned.

"He wants to 'clarify the situation', as he said. But since when does he take the initiative? He didn't say he wanted to apologize for the lousy job he did, almost killing Rodrigo. No, he said we had to meet because things had to be worked out about our relationship in the future. There's no need for a relationship between us. He works for La Migra. We don't. If we need him, we call him."

"What if things have changed, Cesar? What if Tito has other things in mind? I smell something fishy."

"I don't know, Paulo. Maybe there's nothing wrong. Maybe he wants to apologize and clarify what happened. Maybe we shouldn't worry about everything."

"We worry because we have some things we want to keep

hidden. It's our business that makes us worry."

"It's too late for that now. We can't call back the drone. We've got to go forward."

"But you didn't know the merchandise had cocaine in it. How come nobody told you? Who's in charge?"

"Relax! I'm in charge. I've already asked the question, and I'll get the answer. Tito's concerned about the botched up job on Miguel. He's not in the loop for anything else that concerns us."

"I hope you're right. So you're going to show up?"

"Yeah. I just wanted to discuss this with you, Paulo. Now I feel better about it. In any case, now you know. If things go wrong, you know where I went."

"You're taking a chance, Cesar."

"You're a worrywart, Paulo. Relax, you'll live longer."

As Cesar drove away, Paulo decided to act on his instincts. He had always thought Cesar was wrong about Manuel. Sure, Rodrigo was a working ant as Cesar said. He was delivering the merchandise with no questions asked, but Manuel was respected in the Tohono O'odham nation for his clear thinking and honesty. Paulo looked up at the tiny speck above the bajada where Manuel's ramada sat against the rocks. He decided to drive up to it.

Manuel was pampering his motorcycle, polishing the chrome with a soft cloth. His bike was starting to sparkle and he could see himself as in a mirror in the resplendent metal. He was going to ride to town to see Rodrigo. They might release him from the hospital in a couple of days.

The change in his nephew amazed him. This near catastrophe had produced a miraculous change, a change he himself had been unable to produce in his nephew. It must have been a celestial favor.

Manuel still felt off-center, uneasy about their situation. The attempt made by this strange character, El Pato, was a harbinger of more dangerous scenarios for the future. No refuge was high or remote enough to isolate them for very long from unpredictable attacks.

He felt responsible for Rodrigo. He was determined to protect him. At first, it had been more about self-preservation than concern for Rodrigo. He did not want Rodrigo to be shamed; it would tarnish his own reputation. Then events got out of his control. The failed kidnapping, the attempt on Miguel's life that almost killed his nephew, then his own intervention, taking action to dispose of the drugs, produced a transformation. The walls separating him from Rodrigo crumbled. He took the guilt of Rodrigo onto his own shoulders. The attempt on his nephew's life became an attempt on his own. The events blurred the separations. Miguel's fate became his concern. His proud isolation morphed into a union. He and his friends developed a bond that broke barriers, a mysterious flame that burned in them. Even Hank, who had stayed on the borderline of the drug business, was part of this group. And Miguel had shown him a new perspective about people like Lupe, who risked their lives to try to improve the lives of others. His body was not an armor that protected him from the rest of the world. The world leaked into him like sea water through his skin, it became an extension of his body. Even the rocky summit of Baboquivari was his extended family. Maybe even his shiny motorcycle was not just an inanimate object. It had a meaning for him and influenced his life.

The sound of a car climbing to his place drew him from his thoughts. It was a police car. He continued polishing his bike.

"Hola, Manuel, your horse needs new shoes?

"Hola, Paulo! No, just getting it ready to ride. I'm going to go to town to see my nephew. He's in the hospital, you know."

"Yeah, that's a shame, a real shame. When is he going to be released?"

"Not sure. That's what I intend to find out. Now that he's gone, I miss him. You're alone? Where's your twin?"

"He's off on some business. That's why I'm here. Manuel, I need your advice. I believe Cesar's in danger. I told him not to go, but he's stubborn as a jackass, as usual."

"What business is that?"

"He's gone to meet with Tito."

"Who's Tito?"

"He works for La Migra."

"What's wrong with that?"

Paulo hesitated, and scratched his head. "Manuel, the reason I came to you is because I know I can trust you. I have tried to reason with Cesar before, but he never listened and just told me to shut up and follow him. Now, I might as well tell you the whole thing."

"If that's going to help me understand what you want to tell me, go ahead."

"Tito's the one who ordered the drone strike that hit Rodrigo."

"What? Why would he do that?" demanded Manuel. "Does he know Rodrigo?"

"Let me tell you a bit more. The target was Miguel. But they loused it up. Tito was in charge, and he loused it up, and the drone went for Rodrigo instead. It was all a big screw up."

"Why go after Miguel? What did he do?"

"That's what I told Cesar. I told him he didn't have any proof that Miguel was involved. But Cesar was sure, he said, that Miguel had intercepted the shipment of cocaine Rodrigo had received. He said Miguel was a member of the drug cartel and had decided to bypass him, Cesar, and was trying to take over. So he wanted to punish him and recover the merchandise. He was after Miguel. He wanted to have him killed. So he thought about using Tito, and had Tito order a strike against Miguel, using the drone. But something went wrong. Instead of Miguel, it locked on Rodrigo and went for him."

"Wait, Paulo. You're too fast for mi cabesa. What does Cesar have to do with cocaine trafficking? How's he mixed up with drugs?"

"That's the ugly part of this, Manuel. That's why I have to trust you. Rodrigo, when he picked up merchandise, was working for Cesar, and I was in it too. Now Rodrigo knew nothing about that, he just picked up and delivered. And believe me, please, Manuel, Cesar and I were looking after your nephew, making sure nothing bad happened. He didn't know we were part of the organization, and we couldn't tell him!"

"Oh, I see. You and Cesar were doing him a favor by letting him get involved with drugs? He told me it was pot, and you guys do him a favor by giving him two hundred kilos of pot mixed with cocaine!"

"Believe me, Manuel, we didn't know there was cocaine. We were as surprised as Rodrigo. When Cesar heard about it, he was furious. He wanted to stop the deal, but it was too late. Then Rodrigo refused to deliver it, and Miguel appears out of nowhere and everybody thought he was the mastermind. Even El Pato thought so. When he tried to stop you on the road it was to get the merchandise back."

"Who is this El Pato? What was his role?"

"He was at the receiving end. He was to deliver the merchandise to agents in Phoenix."

"And you're policemen? You should be the ones shot at, not my nephew."

"I took a risk in coming to see you, Manuel, but I believe you can help."

"How?"

"I wager that this guy, Tito, is not trying to apologize to Cesar. He's involved in this, much more than it looks. He accepted to direct the strike against Miguel because he knew about the deal, the cocaine, and where it was seen last. It seems Cesar and I were the only dummies left out. I'm sure Tito's directly involved in this new deal. Cesar always refused to deal with cocaine. Tito's taking over. I suspect Tito wants to see Cesar to read him the new rules. What's bad is that, if Tito is one of the drug cartel, they'll want the two hundred kilos back, at any cost. They know you and Rodrigo were involved to some degree. My guess is Cesar's going to be forced to make you return their merchandise. If you can't, it's bad, because the cartel doesn't accept failure. You deliver or you're eliminated. Cesar didn't deliver so he has to be eliminated, and so will you, and Rodrigo, and me too. You're in this mess with us. That's why I came. Maybe the two of us can do something. Let's help each other."

"What do you have in mind?"

"I'm not sure. I can read a situation better than Cesar, but when it comes to action, Cesar always decides."

Manuel thought about Rodrigo recuperating in the hospital. If he did nothing, his nephew's life would be in danger. Rodrigo was an easy target. He thought of his service revolver carefully stashed away. He could start carrying it. But he didn't know who the enemy was, so it would be useless.

"Where's Cesar going to meet Tito?"

"At La Cienega Del Coyote, in less than an hour. We have to do something right away."

Manuel remembered that place as the point of departure of

cattle to be brought to the slaughterhouse in the old days. He went there occasionally to collect cattle skulls and horns that could be found there. A place of doom. "Let's go to that place of doom," Manuel decided. Paulo was taken aback. "To do what?"

"I'm going to have a talk with Tito."

"Are you nuts? You're walking into his trap. Tito chose that place because it's safe for what he wants to do, which is no good. He could kill you, and Cesar too."

"That's why you're taking me there. If anything happens, you're a witness and you can make sure he is brought to justice."

"You won't find any justice there, Manuel. Don't go."

"I'm not counting on Tito's justice, Paulo. It's God's justice I'm counting on. I have to go."

"What do you expect?"

"Nothing of my own. I'm expecting everything to be provided by celestial favors."

"And me, what do I do?"

"You do the same, Paulo."

Paulo drove to within a quarter of a mile of the entrance to La Cienega Del Coyote. Manuel got out of the car and walked the rest of the way. Paulo lost sight of him as he approached the entrance.

A great fear overtook Paulo. He knew he had to do something, but he tried to block it out of his mind. He felt panicky. He grabbed the two-way radio and almost pressed the talk button to call for help, but then he asked himself what he was going to say. He would have to say something like this: "Cesar and I have been importing drugs for months, and lately it has been cocaine. We fooled everybody except the drug cartel. Now they are going to kill Cesar, Manuel, and Rodrigo, and I,

Paulo, am sitting here in my police car like a jackass, not knowing what to do, and I'm panicking. Come help me." He let go of the radio and waited until his mind cleared.

Manuel got to the fallen gate. A Border Patrol van was there, with two other cars parked next to it. He stepped through the gate.

A short and narrow canyon led into La Cienega Del Coyote, a circular opening into the foothills of the Quinlan Mountains, where rainfall during the summer monsoon downpours was gathered into a marsh that fed abundant grass for some weeks. Manuel looked up at the ridge tops enclosing this private world.

He had not noticed before how they delimited an almost perfectly circular area. Every step took him toward center stage, where the shrine stood. He did not see anybody except the statue of La Guadalupe.

From behind the shrine, a head bobbed up, then another, then a third. Tito, Mario, and Cesar had seen him coming and had crouched down beyond the semicircular wall. He felt an icy tingling down his spine. He saw that one of them had a gun in his hand and was pointing it at Cesar's chest. Things had not gone smoothly between Tito and Cesar. Tito, holding the gun, broke through the formalities of introduction. "Bienvenido, Manuel! We were just talking about you, and Cesar was very stubborn. He refused to invite you to join our conversation. But here you are! Cesar had already invited you? I should have guessed. Pardon my ignorance."

"I didn't invite anybody," Cesar defended himself.

"That's right. He didn't," confirmed Manuel.

"I see. You want me to believe that you were just coming for a visit to the shrine, right?"

Manuel had not visited the shrine in years. Standing in front of La Guadalupe, at the center of the circle, he felt totally powerless and somewhat ashamed, like an actor who had forgotten his lines.

"But you're very welcome. I have gathered all your friends to convince you to come."

Tito looked back at the mesquite trees. "Come forward, friends of Manuel. He came on his own. Come see him."

Manuel saw with great sadness that Hank and wife and daughter were there, under the threat of Tito's gun. This was going to be for all the marbles, not just for Rodrigo and Cesar anymore. He felt he was the only one who could still do something. And how many they were... he looked up at the ridge again. There, standing all around, were hundreds of people waiting for him to take action. Rodrigo was there, and Roger and Miguel with their wives. There were people with knapsacks on their backs and water bottles hanging from their belts. There were women with infants in their arms. All looking at him as he stood facing them, paralyzed with fear, unable to think about what to do. Only a celestial favor could change the situation.

"I'm here to ask you a few questions, Tito," Manuel blurted out, trying to regain his composure. "Can you introduce me to the other gentleman? I haven't met him yet."

"Oh, I see. You're here to ask questions?" Tito mocked him. "Let me introduce you to my assistant, Mario, a real gentleman. He's the one that brought your friends here. Now let me tell you a few things. Around here, I'm the one who asks questions. So let's get to the facts. Where's the shipment that belongs to me? I know it was in your possession."

"If you're asking what I did with the cocaine, you'll never see it again. It's at the bottom of a chasm, inside a cave, several hundred feet down. I got rid of it. There is water at the bottom of the chasm. There is no hope of ever getting it out. Nobody can get down there and bring it back up."

"That's very unfortunate for you and for your friends. If you think we're going to write it off as a business loss, you're badly mistaken, Señor Manuel. As a matter of fact, it's very bad for your young nephew, who mishandled the shipment while he had it. We'll take care of him later."

"What do you want with us? There's nothing we can do about your shipment anymore."

"You're correct, Manuel, and that's your bad luck. There's nothing more I can do with you, so you're useless to me, as useless as this shrine. It serves no purpose."

Manuel could feel his presence had a purpose, that what he was going to do would determine the fate of his friends. If only he had brought his own gun, he'd have had a chance. This relying on celestial favors was fraying his nerves. He looked at Hank, who was clutching Kim and Celine tightly and watching him. The only thing was to buy time.

"The shrine will always have a purpose. It ties men to God by inviting them to pray. You should pray too, Tito."

"You sound like somebody I used to know. El Pato was his name. Last time I saw him, he refused to be called El Pato. He insisted I call him Xavier Diaz. But I gave him another name. I called him a useless pawn. You too are useless pawns to me. You're not assets. You're liabilities."

Manuel looked at the shrine for help. La Guadalupe pressed down on the head of the ancient serpent, the enemy of mankind. She was looking slightly off, behind Manuel, toward the fallen gate at the entrance to the canyon. Manuel turned in that direction, following her eyes. There was a column of smoke there, as if a fire had started to burn. Strange. Who would start a fire in this place? Manuel looked back at La Guadalupe. She was serene, fully trusting that her presence there, at the center of the circle, her acceptance of her role, was all that was needed.

Manuel recalled something Kino said. "Out of great catastrophes, greater favors emerge." He said that all it takes is for somebody to receive the favors and pass them on, and they will spread through the desert and propagate to whole nations. "If you start trusting in Providence, the nation stops decaying, and is cleansed by fire. Recognize the celestial favor offered to you."

He looked back to the canyon gate. He could see like flames leaping in the dry grass and attacking the rocks. He murmured to himself, "Let it be now, let it start with me."

Tito, who had been on the right side of the shrine, moved to the left and ordered Manuel and Cesar, at gunpoint, to move to where he had been standing. Cesar was not stable on his feet. Manuel moved slowly and deliberately, to let the column of smoke and the flames take over.

"Señores, I can't say it has been a pleasure to know you, but at least I have been frank with you. I asked you to cooperate. Unfortunately, you're in a position where you can't cooperate usefully. So now I regret but I have to..."

A shot rang out, fired from some distance, and ricocheted off the rocks fifty feet behind the men. Tito paled and looked around. Mario yelled, "La Migra!" and started to run.

"Stay where you are, Mario, I give the orders here!" Tito shouted, turning toward him. But Mario did not stop. Tito did not hesitate. He aimed carefully and fired. Mario fell, tried to get up, but fell back to the ground. Tito aimed at him again, but suddenly fell on his knees and blood gushed from the back of his head, just as the delayed sound of a second shot was heard. Whoever had fired was on target this time.

La Cienega del Coyote had not seen so many visitors in decades. The Tohono O'odham police were outnumbered by Border Patrol and people of all sorts from as far away as Sells.

Border Patrol was appalled that one of their own was an agent of a Mexican drug cartel.

Paulo was becoming a hero. He was explaining again how he'd followed Manuel, bringing his sniper rifle, and hid behind a rock above the gate. He'd waited for Tito to move away from Cesar and Manuel. After the first shot went off target, he quickly adjusted his sight and squeezed another shot. This time he hit the bull's eye.

Cesar was a virtuoso at explaining the events and giving them his own flavor. Tito, he told the investigators and news people who had flocked to the scene of the multiple shooting, had asked him to give a hand in arresting a drug cartel member. So he, Cesar, had set up his spotters along the route and soon got a report that the suspect was walking alone around San Miguel. Cesar then called Tito and gave him the coordinates. Tito suddenly changed his mind and declared that the man was of no interest—it was a mistake. He asked Cesar to let the man go his way. Cesar and Paulo had become suspicious and had hidden to continue the surveillance. Out of the blue, a drone appeared and flew over the place the man was hiding. The drone then took off toward the top of the bajada and fired at somebody.

"As everybody knows by now," explained Cesar, "Rodrigo was nearly killed in the dirty play imagined by Tito. Soon after, Tito contacted me and asked us to meet him so he could explain his dealings with the drone."

By now Cesar was alert to Tito's game, surmising Tito himself was involved in drug dealing. When Tito insisted that Cesar should invite Manuel to a meeting to explain the incident that caused Rodrigo's misadventure, Cesar refused. But then Tito kidnapped Manuel's friends and brought them to the place of desolation.

"Ask Hank and his wife," Cesar invited the crowd. The couple confirmed that they had been lured, with their daughter, into a van and driven here against their will. Satisfied, Cesar continued with his saga. He got the call from Tito and went to meet him.

The rest was history. Paulo talked Manuel into coming to their help. Paulo followed Manuel and with a masterful shot put an end to the double agent who had already killed two of his aides.

People, impressed, congratulated Cesar and Paulo for their skills and astuteness.

With the deaths of Tito, El Pato, and Mario, all traces of the drug cartel had been eliminated. The drone incident that almost killed Rodrigo could now be explained. Thanks to Paulo's marksmanship and Cesar's expertise at weaving a plausible tale, all the blame was shifted onto those who had been killed. As for Rodrigo, Cesar made him out to be an innocent bystander who got wounded, and to compensate for his misfortune, Cesar suggested that Rodrigo be offered a job either with Border Patrol or the local police. The more Cesar and Paulo talked, the more they took center stage. They were to make depositions to all the authorities. There was talk of promotions for both.

Manuel looked around at the crowd and decided to sneak away quietly. He saw Hank and Kim holding hands and walking toward him. Celine was riding on her daddy's shoulders.

"Thanks for showing up, Manuel," said Hank. "I was losing faith in celestial favors until I saw you coming."

"That's about the time I started to lose my own confidence," sighed Manuel. " I felt like the cattle that used to be driven from here to the slaughterhouse. I was running out of ideas when the shots rang out."

"You came, and that made the difference. You risked your life for us. I'll never forget it, Manuel."

"Me neither," affirmed Kim, and she put her arms around her husband. "Hank," she added, "I think I would like to join your choir now."

Manuel walked to the shrine, kissed his hand and touched the Virgin's head. He proceeded to walk with Hank and Kim toward Paulo's car. As he walked through the gate he stopped and looked back. The people on top of the rocks had disappeared. The place had regained its usual appearance.

But to Manuel the Cienega del Coyote had changed. The rocks, the canyon, the dried up marsh and the shrine, and his friends, and even the strangers who had become witnesses of his transformation had entered his heart. They were now part of an immense choir that sang in many different voices, but in harmony, the praises of Providence. The time for the wildfire had come. It would flash through the desert, though cities, nations, and continents, breaking down barriers and uniting all singers.

The End

About The Author

Bruno Jambor

Bruno Jambor is a scientist and engineer. He spent his career in aerospace, designing manned and unmanned spacecrafts to study stars, planets, and the earth's resources. He has a PhD in astronomy.

Bruno Jambor was born in Hungary and resided in France in his early years. He arrived in Chicago at the age of twenty. He graduated from the University of Illinois in mathematics and continued with graduate studies in astronomy.

To finance part of his studies, he worked as a laboratory technician in a Chicago hospital, helping with research about heart disease conducted on dogs. He was a guinea pig on early techniques to automate analysis of electrocardiograms. He was one of the first human subjects whose EKG was sent over phone lines from Chicago to Denver, with results sent back to Chicago. Part of his heartbeats must have stayed in Colorado, because he spent the rest of his career there. While finishing his thesis, he was called out west for a job interview he never applied for and was hired, while his other carefully investigated leads did not work out. Convinced that Providence is much more effective than human planning, he moved his family to the Rocky Mountain state and settled there.

Bruno and his wife Pat live at the foot of the Rockies, where the deer and the antelopes play, but the skies are getting less clear at night due to city lights. He writes and enjoys cultivating what the deer let him grow, which is mostly pinion pine, penstemon, and sage.

ASSASSINS OF ALAMUT

BY

JAMES BOSCHERT

An Epic Novel of Persia and Palestine in the Time of the Crusades

The Assassins of Alamut is a riveting tale, painted on the vast canvas of life in Palestine and Persia during the 12th century.

On one hand, it's a tale of the crusades—as told from the Islamic side—where Shi'a and Sunni are as intent on killing Ismaili Muslims as crusaders. In self-defense, the Ismailis develop an elite band of highly trained killers called Hashshashin whose missions are launched from their mountain fortress of Alamut.

But it's also the story of a French boy, Talon, captured and forced into the alien world of the assassins. Forbidden love for a princess is intertwined with sinister plots and self-sacrifice, as the hero and his two companions discover treachery and then attempt to evade the ruthless assassins of Alamut who are sent to hunt them down.

It's a sweeping saga that takes you over vast snow-covered mountains, through the frozen wastes of the winter plateau, and into the fabulous cites of Hamadan, Isfahan, and the Kingdom of Jerusalem.

"A brilliant first novel, worthy of Bernard Cornwell at his best."—Tom Grundner

PENMORE PRESS
www.penmorepress.com

Historical fiction and nonfiction
Paperback available for order on line
and as Ebook with all major distributers

www.ingramcontent.com/pod-product-compliance
Lightning Source LLC
Chambersburg PA
CBHW070635170726
48291CB00003B/1024